ALLAN CAMERON was bor[illegible] ia
and East Pakistan (later B[illegible] :n
and then started his edu[illegible] at
twenty moved to Italy, w[illegible] ie
trades he has been a Jack of and not mastered include postman, labourer, factory worker, forwarding clerk, hydrographic surveyor and university lecturer. For the last ten years he has finally settled down on the Isle of Lewis, where he writes and translates.

He has published articles in the daily newspaper *L'Unità*, the Italian current affairs magazine *Reset*, and the academic journals *Teoria Politica* and *Renaissance Studies*. He has translated some seventeen books by a variety of writers, including the Italian philosopher, Norberto Bobbio, the president of the European Commission, Romano Prodi, and the leading historian Eric Hobsbawm.

The Golden Menagerie

ALLAN CAMERON

Luath Press Limited
EDINBURGH
www.luath.co.uk

First Published 2004

The paper used in this book is recyclable. It is made from low-chlorine pulps produced in a low-energy, low-emission manner from renewable forests.

The publisher acknowledges subsidy from

Scottish Arts Council

towards the publication of this volume.

Printed and bound by
DigiSource UK Ltd, Livingston
Typeset in Sabon 11 by Sarah Crozier, Nantes

For Margaret, Francesco Alasdair,
Aonghas Gianluca and Flora

Preface

A LITERARY AGENT to whom I submitted this work confided on meeting me that I did not seem as odd as my book. This could mean either that she found me disappointingly dull or that she thought this novel the product of a deranged mind. Possibly she believed both of these things. However, I could perhaps defend myself against the charges by blaming it all on the man who wrote *The Golden Ass* some eighteen centuries ago. In spite of the fact that his book is explicitly anti-Christian both in tone and content, it not only survived in Christian Europe, it flourished. Down through the centuries it has been translated and plagiarised. In English we have William Adlington's splendid sixteenth-century translation and Robert Graves' uncharacteristically and unnecessarily prosaic version. Boccaccio plundered the work for his *Decameron*, Chaucer must have felt its influence and the sixteenth-century Italian writer, Agnolo Firenzuola, even wrote his own updated version of *The Golden Ass* set in contemporary Tuscany. But Apuleius could have used my same defence, as Graves points out in the introduction to his translation: 'He probably invented none of his stories, though it is clear that he improved them'. He in turn must have used Lucius of Patra's *The Ass* or Lucian of Samosata's *Lucius, or the Ass*.

Robert Graves is right to stress that Apuleius' version is a religious work dedicated to the cult of Isis. However, I do not share his belief that the account of Lucius' conversion to the cult after returning to his human form 'is a real and moving one'. The rituals of a kind of second-century freemasonry are dull and rather unattractive, but the rest of the work is cleverly narrated and does put forward a moral code, although not one that most of us would find very inspiring. Graves tells us that the three main moral precepts of Apuleius' religion are: 1. Inequality: slaves and freedmen cannot aspire to all human virtues, and anything that encourages this is inimical to good order; 2. Ill-luck is contagious: while not being needlessly cruel, a virtuous man should not lose time with anyone who has fallen on hard times, as this could then rebound on him; 3. The supernatural is dangerous and should not be meddled with, and this belief appears to have resulted in a terror of 'dark forces'. It also survived in Christian Europe, most notably in the widespread tradition of the 'evil eye'.

We then have to ask ourselves why a text that refers to Christianity contemptuously as a 'slave religion' should continue to be so successful after that religion attains the full backing of the state. Graves makes much of St. Augustine's loathing of Apuleius, who coincidently was born in Madaura (in what is now Morocco) very close to where the Saint was to be born. But the state religion that he subscribed to was no longer the radical one of Apuleius' time. Predestination re-established order and hierarchy, and his dislike of Gnostic sects was much greater than his dislike of Apuleius' Isis. Indeed Isis now lived on in the cult of the Virgin Mary, another syncretic addition. Yet it would be wrong to say that Christianity had not changed morality. Graves contrasts Augustine's shame over his previous fascination for the amphitheatre with Apuleius' honourable old age in which 'he organised the gladiatorial and wild-beast shows for the whole province of Africa', although it is hard to agree with Graves' implication that this meant Apuleius was therefore the more balanced and possibly even the better of the two men.

I know nothing about early Christian attitudes to sexuality, but it strikes me that Christianity as an established state religion shared a very similar view to that of Apuleius, and that is why he continued to be read. Fotis, who is the cause of his character's metamorphosis, is the original evil temptress. The genre was consistently anti-feminist (if you can be 'anti' something that has not yet been invented). This was the starting point for my novel: a new version had to create a woman who is not the cause of the central character's downfall but his saviour. The man has to become responsible for his own mistakes and sufferings; the woman has to be stronger, wiser and possibly even nobler, in the more restricted sense of nobility that accords with my version, which is essentially egalitarian.

Why resurrect a genre that appears to have had a doubtful past and to have run its course? Once the evil temptress has been jettisoned, the story of the *Golden Ass* appears relevant for several reasons. Firstly, absurd transformations into animals seem more relevant now we are becoming increasingly aware of how we are much more part of the animal world than Christian and humanist traditions led us to believe. Secondly, the cult of mirth satirised by Apuleius is more significant today, because there are very few things we take seriously. The best humour thrives on adversity, whereas humour that has no taboos to challenge is often a little superficial. I do not wish to criticise our cynicism too harshly, as it is preferable to the fanaticism that has often marred the Modern Era, nor do I want to sound moralistic. This genre hopefully allows me to satirise our mindless hedonism without falling into those traps. Thirdly, when it works well, this kind of writing can bring together the profane, the noble, the perverse, the paradoxical and above all uncertainty (Apuleius, Boccaccio, Rabelais and perhaps even Chaucer are all writers who seem unable to determine their religiosity, and it is only our knowledge of their lives that can confirm that they were in fact religious). It creates room for both symbolic and rational discourse. It is the plate brimming with a wide variety of foods, the *satura lanx* from which we derive the word 'satire'. Fourthly and most importantly, it creates an opportunity for the action best described by the Italian verb *sbizzarrirsi*, which is rendered rather disappointingly in English as 'to run riot' or 'to indulge oneself'. Apuleius clearly understood the stylistic freedom enjoyed by a writer of *transformations*. Nobody could put it better than Graves:

> Why did Apuleius choose to write in this eccentric style? For the same reason that Rabelais did. The parallel is close. Both were priests – pious, lively, exceptionally learned, provincial priests – who found that the popular tale gave them a wider field for their descriptions of contemporary morals and manners, punctuated by philosophical asides, than any more respectable literary form.

Today most western readers, like me, have only a very rudimentary understanding of Latin, so not only can we not read Apuleius' original, we cannot appreciate the stylistic subtleties, as Graves could. I am therefore loath to challenge him on the problems of rendering the original Latin into modern English. However, I cannot understand his decision to make 'no attempt to bring out the oddness of the Latin'. It seems to me that a certain stylistic quirkiness is essential, if this type of literature is to achieve its artistic aims, or to use the jargon, its method of defamiliarisation. Graves may have meant that modern English has become an extraordinarily rigid language, quite different to the one used by Adlington.

I would also like to acknowledge my small debt to Bao Ninh's novel, *The Sorrow of War*, whose lively and effective English translation provides us with probably the best analysis of the Vietnam War in literature or film, as well as a denunciation of war and a great love story. My narrative is different, as mine is just a small motif to stress that human beings are after all something more than an animal and are indeed capable of great selflessness. I was also looking for something to parallel to Apuleius' story of *Cupid and Psyche*, although again with a very different purpose. I use the characters' names from *The Sorrow of War*, partly because I do not know many Vietnamese names and partly because I would like to 'pay homage' to an excellent novel.

Finally, this genre lends itself to scepticism, and this is probably why it has also been used by the pious. It allowed them to express doubts they possibly did not even wish to admit to themselves. I, on the other hand, have no rigid religious beliefs to herald at the end of the novel, so in place of Apuleius' high priests I have concluded with three dialogues. The dialogue has survived elsewhere, but in English we have for some time ignored its potential (particularly for sceptical and satirical discourse). In English, it is a genre that we have to learn again to read and write.

I think it was the correct decision to write this short explanatory preface, especially as I dislike the twentieth century's elitist preference for obscurantism for the sake of obscurantism, but I would also hope that this book can be enjoyed without knowing anything I have mentioned in these few introductory pages.

Allan Cameron
Isle of Lewis, January 2004

CHAPTER ONE

My First Metamorphosis

The author undergoes a terrible transformation, sets off to experience life as a quadruped, and learns to distrust anyone who says there is any meaning to life.

To be the offspring of a taut-strung state
the rigid regiment of thought, and fate
held in its distant godhead nation,
invisible soul of petty machination,
is my desire.

For then could I well justify the fire
that burns when the wideness of the world
the child perceived is shrunken by the lanky limbs
of youth to whom the sullen meanness is unfurled
by reaching above the parapet of parental trust,
distance diminished by the distant view
of crowded commonplace,
discovered the joy of the joyless face.

For then could I give vent
to all the pent-up anger against the castle
constructed on the shifting sands,
tear at the wall with bleeding hands,
believe in better worlds, built and buttressed
by our solid dreams, by the martyred word
of truth upholding the absurd.

'THERE IS A POINT to all this,' said the woman that I wanted to bed. It was the first time that her shape, her smell and her pheromonal intensity had appeared before me, but such is the capricious, indiscriminate and sudden nature of the young male of our species, whose lust can take flight in its fantasies like a vigorous bird of prey, although its actual physical manifestation may be more akin to the apparently random and mindless exuberance of a March hare. Erratic, ridiculous and vaguely pitiful, given the expenditure of energy. She had been standing there patiently while the others spoke earnestly in long, convoluted and over-enthusiastic sentences that wound around you like sticking tape and ignored the average concentration span. They were God-botherers, meaning-of-life salespeople or something like that. They had some philosophy to sell. And they would have knocked at the wrong door, if it had not been for her, a warm smile, a woman, who, simply for being that, I now wished to pass intimate moments with. They had knocked at the wrong door because I cared about nothing in this world, not about global-warming, not about overpopulation, not about genetically modified vegetables, not about the Second Coming, and not about truth, goodness and a better life, but they had knocked at the right one in that I was easy bait, a sucker for soft eyes and a soft voice.

I was, then, a feeble and pathetic figure. I still am, but now I know that everyone else is too. Then I thought I was the only feeble and pathetic figure in a world populated by heroes. A lonely existence? Perhaps, but also a more exciting one, because I expected more of others and wanted more of myself.

I was a tall, lanky, awkwardly jointed envelope of human flesh, which had just completed, at least from a legal point of view, that long and tedious process called childhood. How can I dress up the banality of my background? Can I possibly interest you in someone born in Croydon? My father, whose duties for a company that imported bathroom accessories I never fully understood, was a man who concentrated all his energies into the development of total indifference, an art so well-exercised that it was by then almost instinctive. Nothing in the world, even in the less significant world of our standard, four-membered nuclear family, ever touched the majesty of his intellectual isolation. He may, however, once have been different – long before when my infant mind could not have assessed him – for my mother always held him responsible for my somewhat eccentric first name: Lucian.

I suppose I should speak of my sister. I had, I confess, considered ignoring her altogether. As she has no particular relevance to the strange events I am going to describe, I could quite easily have exercised my artistic license and claimed to be an only child. But a gap in the truth is a lie, and she was important for what she was not. She was not me. And the truth is that I am loath to speak of her, her superficial cleverness, the cat-like way she slithered into adult life and made herself so comfortable. Adult? At sixteen, she didn't have my newly acquired right to vote, but she required and seemed to receive the respect of that composed, responsible and ordered adult world that refused to embrace me to its fold. I will not speak of her academic successes too painful to recount. When I had been at school, I had really been at school, enclosed within the limitations of my schoolboy existence, but she would return from school with the same aplomb that my father would return from his office, carrying the purposefulness of her busy day and the weight of her future ambitions. She would dress smartly and was then taken out by her boyfriend, an equally virtuous expression of modern youth. Being a computer programmer, he must have run a programme to compute the nature of a desirable partner and found that the result equalled my sister or someone very like her. He looked a man who always knew the right thing to do in every situation that life or fate presented him with. He drove a sporty but not too sporty automobile, a vehicle that extended his power over time and space, that presented itself like a well-tamed animal, sharing his clean-cut lifestyle.

So I have presented myself, I have outlined something of my ambivalent nature, the humility and the arrogance: the lack of desire to do anything, together with the desire to take life by assault, to conquer new heights. I wanted to be different from my father and my future brother-in-law, without having any idea of what the substance of that difference should be. Difference for difference's sake, like the shock of pink Mohican hair that rose from my stubbly scalp. I am a child of my time, and this is the parable of the *zeitgeist*. Inconclusive.

It was a wintry and overcast summer's evening when those strangers came to my door. Who they were is still unclear to me. They unpackaged truths with insincere verve, and felt sure that I was in need of them – of their clear, crisp, synthetic ideas that cranked away in tasteless certitude. I was momentarily a challenge, the centre of interest – a mental landscape that needed to be conquered and colonised. I was possibly not the most interesting or exotic conquest, more of an infertile desert, uninhabited by any beliefs, convictions or indeed specific ambitions. My emptiness had rarely attracted such interest, and I felt a confused mixture of flattery and diffidence. My eyes were fixed on that single female member of the party, whose name, as I would learn later, was Fotis. As they spoke, her mouth broadened into sweet reassurance; as they argued, a millimetric movement of her breast sent shudders of pleasure down my back. They remonstrated to deaf ears, while her body spoke to my libido.

They invited me to a meeting, and in a hypnotic daze I climbed into a dark, dark-windowed limousine and swept through the rectangular grid of the housing estate, through other endless, formless streets from which drives and pathways splayed, leading down like wires through doors and corridors to individuals that lit their own loves, passions and desires, and continued predictably towards their own ends in crowded solitudes. The lights of the windows marked where groups of lives followed these tragic trajectories, of which I knew nothing but their certain existence. Occasionally they were switched off and met the darkness of the night. Behind each light were people similar to me, and yet so different in that they were not me and my experiences, as I spun from harsh reality to the harsher nightmare of the fantastic. Finally we came to a white, church-like building, stark, modern, uninviting. Inside, however, it was far from church-like: strange symbols hung on the walls, their arcane meanings contrasted with their plastic fabrication. It was unclear whether these symbols were purposefully kitsch and thus expressions of an evolved and erudite sense of humour, or merely bad taste and thus expressions of some obscure faith, concealing the threat of an unpredictable fanaticism. An energetic bald-headed man, whose obesity seemed in no way to impair his agility, was clearly in charge, and with guru self-conceit he instructed Fotis to go to the kitchen. I followed in a trance. Inside, I stroked the delicious circle of her left buttock with a sweaty and trembling hand. She swung round as though surprised that I had followed her, and after a second in which her face expressed incomprehension, she softened suddenly, sweetly, and smiled. 'Tonight' she said, 'in the bell tower, after the ceremony'. Her voice (which I heard for the first time) revealed itself deeper than expected, authoritative, delightful. She looked at me with a touch of pity, as one might look at someone who has unknowingly been chosen for an unpleasant fate, and put an index finger to her lips, suggesting that my behaviour might not have met with the full approval of the rest of the company, whom she intimated me to rejoin. The pity in her expression was one of many signals that, in my besotted state, I decided to ignore.

You can now imagine my excitement and how I now hated the unknown ceremony that separated me from Fotis' embraces. After the terrifying adventures that ensued that night, I was tempted to blame her for all my sufferings. Had I not been so possessed by lustful infatuation, my reason might have been sufficiently active to avoid my being exposed to public ridicule. Had I not been ridiculed, I might not have attempted to acquire the power of magic. Desire before a fall, and pride the product of a near escape. I do not blame Fotis for the indignities I was about to suffer that evening or as a result of my horrific mutations. She gave me no encouragement, and I believe she wished me no harm. I returned to the main hall which was filling with people. I had clearly happened upon the company of some strange sect engaged in one of its regular and ritualistic meetings. I alone seemed unaware of the rules of this strange society. I looked about for Fotis and saw her reassuring shape darting from one group to another, carrying a tray of drinks. The room buzzed with a strange kind of excitement and people were talking simply to fill up time, their minds fixed firmly on the ceremony. The guests were all eccentrically dressed but not overly so. It was by no means fancy dress, rather the dress of those who care about their appearance and wish to be slightly different. For the most part they were well-spoken, slightly affected, actors perhaps; slight eccentricity was their convention.

The door at the end of the hall opened and in stepped the bald-headed guru. Fancy dress indeed. I have always been untouched by ritual; my prosaic nature can only perceive the limited stature of those who portray grandeur. The wide-girthed guru was wearing only a swimming costume, a quantity of plastic vine wrapped around his shoulders and belly and on his head a brightly coloured, papier-mâché cornucopia. The crowd opened like the Red Sea to give him passage and started to chant 'Hail Bacchus', some in an embarrassed mutter, some with ironic exaggeration, some with wild fervour. On arriving at the centre of the room, he raised his hand for silence and spoke:

'We are gathered together to celebrate mirth and laughter, song and dance, wine and spirit. Mirth renews our tiring souls, laughter regenerates our flagging brains, song enhances emotions oft forgot, dance unwinds muscles tensed by drudgery, and wine and spirits release diabolic inhibitions on our desires. Come, we must feast!' And like a Hollywood actor he strode across to the banqueting tables, to the ensuing applause.

While it is true that laughter is a powerful weapon against pomposity, the bald-headed Bacchus had just proved that pomposity is an equally powerful weapon against laughter. I followed.

Now that I have read some of the Greek authors, I very much doubt that the ancients feasted Bacchus in quite that fashion. The English can only learn to relax at table after having travelled extensively abroad where they have to unlearn the inhibiting effects of a rigid social regime called table manners. The most inhibiting part of these rules of etiquette is that nobody is quite sure what they are. When conversation is naturally stilted and earnest, it is difficult to affect revelry.

I attacked my scampi with the glee of those on limited disposable income who find themselves in a situation of unexpected luxury free from the impending certainty of the bill and nagging uncertainty over the amount. And as I concentrated on this important task, a man wearing a pince-nez interrupted me with the affected tones that could only be expected of a man wearing a pince-nez: 'Young man, I envy you a great deal'. Having made this weighty statement, he stared at me with enlarged black irises through the twin orbits of his pince-nez, waiting patiently for my inevitable and somewhat feeble 'Why is that?'

'Yes indeed, why? Can't you guess, my young friend? Can't you see that you, penniless as you are, possess the one thing that all these wealthy people desire and cannot buy, and indeed that you cannot sell even if you were fool enough to want to? You cannot sell the spring to the autumn, you can only wait for new seed to flower.'

I had strong doubts about the stability of the brain that stared out through the pince-nez, nor could I be bothered to fathom the enigmas and circumlocutions with which he spoke, but I tried to humour him with smiles in the short intervals between spooning the slightly insipid scampi into my mouth.

'He envies your youth' interpreted a bald man sitting next to him, 'in so many words he is simply saying that he would like to start his life over again'.

'Oh, right,' I replied, finding it hard to sympathise with the problem.

'Only Mirth enhances our dull lives, and Mirth has a marked preference for the young' said the mirthless owner of the pince-nez. 'It is one of life's great ironies that the young who have the physical constitution to achieve real pleasure are not intellectually mature enough to appreciate it fully.'

'Youth is not always hedonistic' returned the bald head, 'often it is overly zealous. But you isolate mirth and by doing so you make it artificial. Bacchus was indeed a great god, but only one of many gods. Alone in a materialistic world he has become a bloated and lonely old man, who drinks not out of pleasure but out of sadness for his friends who have passed away. And not only for his friends but also for his enemies.'

'What enemies?'

'The puritans of course. Bacchus' greatest pleasure was to rile the puritans and make the hypocrites uncomfortable.'

'Bacchus requires no antithesis in order to define himself, no opposite that will allow his virtues to shine,' continued the pince-nez. 'Bacchus is the energetic desire to indulge all passions, to conquer life by pleasure. He represents the individual's struggle with himself, not of course to suffocate pleasure as the Stoics and the Christians would have it along with the rest of that rag-bag of philosophers and religious fanatics that history has thrown up. No, Bacchus struggles against the limitations that our bodies and minds put on our appetite for pleasure. Such is human frailty, that even the most seasoned banquet-goer tires after his third banquet in a row, even Don Giovanni must have had some limit to his sexual prowess. Not only do the stimulants we use such as alcohol and drugs take a toll on our mortal frames, but worst of all we tire mentally. Starve us of a pleasure and our desire will grow to a passion, and from a passion to an obsession. Give us free access to that pleasure and in three days we will count it for nothing, we will deride it and start to look for other less accessible pleasures. But immortal Bacchus knows none of this foolishness: when he drinks he is merry but never feels sick, when he makes love he never tires, when he laughs he has joy and never falters, he is convivial but cares for no one and no thing but his pleasure, which he masters perfectly.'

'Unfortunately,' replied the bald head, 'your Bacchus lived before they discovered cholesterol, lung cancer, swollen livers, insomnia and other products of a dissolute life-style (when they heard the word 'dissolute', the diners gasped at such blasphemy, as though to dispute the morality that the word implied). Unfortunately medical science is on the side of the puritans and is a more convincing detractor of your philosophy than all the moralists and bigots put together. But I would go further. According to Newton's theories, if a body is acted upon by a single force, it will disappear off into space travelling at a regular and somewhat monotonous speed in the same direction. If, however, it is acted on by several forces, its trajectory can take on any number of complex configurations, a circle or an ellipse; it may even come to a sublime state of equilibrium. And so it is with us: we are in the midst of many forces and Bacchus is only one of them. He is a good force but only if he does not act alone. As he is the most visible force, many fall into your trap.'

And so they continued, the bald man's heresy and the pince-nez's sombre defence of merriment.

* * * * *

During the evening I had been passed a lottery ticket, and when at the end of the meal the master of ceremonies prepared to declare the winning number, I extracted the ticket from my pocket, and along with all my fellow revellers awaited the outcome with the bored impatience that usually accompanies these events. I am seldom lucky and was unaware of the nature of the winning prize, so I didn't recognise my number when it was shouted. It was my companion with the pince-nez who prompted me: 'That's your number, isn't it?' As I had never shown him my ticket, this knowledge of his should have made me suspicious, but the realisation of my triumph over the laws of probability caused such a rush of blood and alcohol to the brain that I took no notice of this little clue. I stood up, my head dizzy with sensations, unable to focus on the many faces that must have been turned towards me. 'Here it is!' I cried.

'You're a lucky man,' said the wearer of the pince-nez, 'a lucky man indeed'. He was suppressing a smile. Could he really identify so strongly with my success after so short an acquaintance, or did his smile mean something else? I have always been very inept at understanding these things. The bald-head stared at me with something akin to compassion. My prize turned out to be a go on the newly formulated pleasure computer, the latest and ultimate instrument in the battle for hedonism. Every pleasurable experience could be experienced without leaving the cubicle. For that's what they were offering me – a cubicle.

Inside it was just big enough for a small desk, a desk-top computer and a stool. Under the desk there were various hi-tech boxes with LEDs, flashing coloured lights, whirring gigabytes, RAMs that promised startling silicon profundity and the accumulated science of years of research and experiment. The master of ceremonies apologised for the rather improvised appearance of the technology, which was due to its prototypal innovativeness. As he attached an electrode to each of my temples, he assured me that the computer would explain everything: all I had to do was follow the instructions carefully. 'This young man,' he said, 'is to be our intrepid explorer who will chart the new territories of pleasure and return with knowledge of the virtual world.' With an enormous grin he closed the cubicle door. I was alone and happy, certain that this new-found fortune meant a change for the better in my life. I hadn't forgotten Fotis' invitation. I was noticed at last. I was envied. I had won the prize. Fortune had finally decided to lay her hand on me. I had always known it would. I had been chosen.

I looked up at the computer terminal and carefully read the instructions:

WELCOME TO BACCHUS' PLEASURE PALACE
THE COMPLETE SOFTWARE PACKAGE DESIGNED TO BRING YOU EVERY PLEASURE WITHOUT ANY THOUGHT OR EFFORT ON YOUR BEHALF.
Press Y for Menu

I pressed 'Y'.

Congratulations on choosing BACCHUS©
THE COMPLETE SOFTWARE PACKAGE
Press M if you are male and F if you are female

I pressed 'M'.

Enter your age to the nearest year

I entered 18.

CHOOSE ANY OF THE FOLLOWING BACCHIC PLEASURES THE SENSATIONS OF WHICH BACCHUS© WILL TRANSMIT DIRECTLY TO YOUR BRAIN AS IN A DREAM.

1. Sexual intercourse – heterosexual – no dangers of sexually transmitted diseases
2. Sexual intercourse – homosexual – no dangers of sexually transmitted diseases
3. Drunkenness – with no hangovers
4. Four-course meal – with no indigestion
5. The ultimate trip – with no addiction
6. Adulation – without the hassle of having to brown-nose others first
7. Adventure – without real danger to life or limb
8. Voyeurism – without having to strain your eyes
9. Masochism – no lasting pain for your pleasure
10. Sadism – finally a socially acceptable way to indulge your desires

Having already eaten a four-course meal and drunk a certain quantity of alcohol, I thought that 3 and 4 had already been achieved by more old-fashioned methods with the ensuing natural risks to the brain and digestive system. Besides my mood and natural inclination suggested that no.1 would probably have been the better choice. I pressed 1.

It wasn't pleasure that I felt but searing pain. I fell off the stool while agonising pulses throbbed through my brain at regular intervals. It was a few seconds before I realised that I could only stop the pain by tearing off the electrodes. I lay, huddled up on the floor of the cubicle, holding my head between my hands. Their machine clearly had some teething problems – that was no orgasm I had just felt.

When I staggered out of the cubicle, all eyes were on me, but they weren't the admiring eyes that salute the return of an astronaut who has tested the limits of ingenuity, and has been enriched with new experiences to further human knowledge. Their eyes were full of tears, their bodies limp with excessive laughter. Fotis explained to me later that the electrodes could only transmit electric shocks at given intervals, strong enough to cause pain but too weak to cause any lasting damage to the brain. The whole scene had been transmitted to a large video-screen, so they had witnessed my expression of naive anticipation followed by repeated spasms of agony. They had watched me on the floor as I had tried to figure out what was going on. I had been invited for this specific purpose – to be an object of ridicule, the butt of their banana-skin humour. They had not been in search of a convert, but merely a gullible youth on which to avenge their passing years.

'Forgive us,' said Bacchus theatrically extending both arms in a gesture of goodwill, 'forgive our little prank that was in no way directed against you. You are Innocence and we salute you. You have given us the greatest gift of all, mirth, and we thank you for it from the bottom of our hearts.' At this point the guests began to clap and those nearest to me came up, embraced me breathing warm odours of alcoholic bonhomie and patting my back to the rhythm of their convivial grunts. Needless to say the situation was becoming more and more disagreeable by the minute; the blurred smiles of the well-to-do pranksters that thronged around me added to the recent injury the insult of their belated benevolence.

I pushed through the crowd, tears of self-pity welling in my eyes, followed by comments either of moral support or disdain for my inability to play the part of the good sport. I finally made it to the oak door, and out to the cool air of Croydon's wintery summer evening. The grey dome of its sky hung heavy on the greyness of the town. My head felt that pressure as it burst with shame. When I finally closed the door on the mirth worshippers, I found some small solace in breathing a fraction of that heavy expanse that glowed in the artificial light, sticky with carbon monoxide and fumes from the arteries of a great population of busy machines that hurtled buzzing through the furrowed spaces of the city night. Then a smooth hand slipped into mine: 'Have you forgotten me?' came the voice of Fotis, deep but soft and reassuring.

I withdrew my hand instinctively to demonstrate my hurt, but no sooner did it lose contact with hers than I regretted my impulsive self-pity. Fortunately, she pushed her hand back into mine and said: 'Forgive us, it was a pointless prank. Bacchus went too far this time. I'll make it up to you.'

Such simple words, those last ones. Sufficient to quicken my heart and renew a sense of drunkenness, after the sobering effects of being mocked. Fotis led me by the hand to a back entrance into the bell tower, we climbed several flights of steps until we found ourselves in a small room almost completely filled by a double bed. A dense feeling of desire seemed to emanate from Fotis, a desire so warm that it was unaware of the passage of time. The presence of Fotis' body and the movement of her touch seemed to change the very essence of being, the rhythm of lovemaking took over my body of which until that moment I had been unblissfully unaware. I discovered a new dimension to my humanity as I climbed with Fotis the steep gradation of our pleasure.

Fotis' beauty would perhaps have been more appreciated in the eighteenth century. Although she could not be described as fat, she was generously proportioned in all three of the statistics quoted for professional reasons by both dressmakers and journalists of that strange British institution, the tabloid press, which institutionalises and commercialises the libido to the point of destroying it. But even in the eighteenth century, Fotis would have been considered more suitable to labour than to leisure, more likely to laugh at tavern talk than to swoon at a slightly risqué drawing room comment, more probably the amorous apprenticeship of the comic novel's hero than the crowning achievement of matrimony and order re-established. Indeed her beauty would be appreciated in any age, while fashionable beauty is more extreme, like the candid translucence of the Renaissance lady or the sylph-like innocence of a Sixties model. Her beauty was a robust lust for life, a feminine will that inspired.

I fell into a deep sleep, only to be woken some hours later by a movement on the stairs. I reached out for my companion but found that she had gone. I lay still for a couple of minutes while curiosity struggled to overcome prudence and then, having slipped on my pants and shirt, I crept barefoot up the stairs, shuddering at intervals from either cold or fear. I heard movement and strange invocations, I felt I was close to danger, but I could not stop myself from moving forward towards the source of my inquisitiveness. I had to know what she was up to, and I suffered a kind of jealousy for whatever had drawn her away from me. I knew she was my superior in knowledge and experience. I resented that gap between us, but also feared it. The spirals became narrower, more claustrophobic and difficult to climb. My heart pumped out a feeling of nausea that spread around my body. On several occasions, I stopped and considered turning back. I continued not out of bravery, but out of that youthful belief that life really did hold something for me. And that something might well lie at the top of those stairs. After my night with Fotis, I felt like a conquering hero. My mind completely blanked out the humiliation of the previous evening and returned to my moment of triumph, when I had won the draw. I was fortunate and my life was going to change. I was on a roll.

Eventually the many spirals of the increasingly confined spiral staircase opened up into a strange room. It wasn't so much a room as the space where the bell should have been. Three sides of the hybrid room were closed by wooden slats, but the fourth was completely open to the elements and in its arch, silhouetted by the lunar glow, stood Fotis, naked, arms outstretched, calling in some foreign tongue to an obscure deity or spirit. Then she turned and took one of the jars aligned along a shelf and barely lit by the deep tones of the moon's persuasive beams. In a moment I was convinced of the unthinkable presence of other forces – forces of darkness if you like – hidden spirits, insubstantial existences and terrible powers. Fotis took some ointment from the jar and again invoked her spirits. Then the unbelievable started to happen, although I had been prepared for it by the sensation of unreality I had just felt. Fotis began to change. Feathers appeared on her back and on her arms that transformed into graceful wings. Her legs shortened and her feet curled up into vicious claws. She was turning into an eagle.

Just before her metamorphosis was complete, she made her last human utterance, a deep-throated laugh, not satanic, more an expression of her vitality, of her conquest over life. Off she flew with aquiline ease, with graceful leaps along the hidden ladder of the air that she beat beneath those powerful wings. And then she swooped with all the sureness and the joy of the strong. I had always felt a kind of envy for the effortless flight of such birds, but when I knew that in that bird flew a human soul, my desire to follow became feverish, disengaged from the powers of reason. In the gloom, I felt with trembling hands for the right jar. I was sure it was the third one along from the end, I never considered that it may have been another. I took a handful and rubbed it hard around my chest and back. After a second it started to burn, as though caustic; it burnt deep into my flesh. Only then did it occur to me that the ointment might have a result other than the one desired. Not feathers but short, curly, pubic hairs were sprouting all over my body. At first I thought that I was about to take on the form of some primate, but suddenly I was doubled up in agony, excruciating endless agony; my bones were shrinking and changing shape.

I may have lost consciousness; in any event I was soon conscious of having turned into some diminutive quadruped, and my alarmed yelping, which at first I didn't recognise as mine, led me to understand that my new body probably belonged to some canine breed. What was I to do? Surprise, the sheer novelty of my situation kept despair at bay for a short while. I attempted to walk, and found the experience of walking on two legs is no help at all when it comes to walking on four. Should the legs on either side be in step or not? I fell over several times before I learnt the answer. It also takes a great deal of practice to get both the front and back legs to go the same distance. After a quarter of an hour, circling the narrow confines of the bell-less, bell-tower room, I became more adept at the art of four-legged locomotion, and having dealt with that immediate problem, I began to realise the various ramifications of my predicament. If I didn't want to remain a dog for the rest of my life, I had to find the right ointment to change myself back. I could of course have waited and asked Fotis for help on her return. On the other hand I had no idea of how long she went off for on her aquiline escapades, nor could I have foreseen what her reaction would have been to my metamorphosis and whether she would have been inclined to help me.

I set about the business of climbing up to the shelf, leaving the greater problem of deciding which ointment to use until I had overcome this first obstacle. But my reduced strength was unequal to the task of pushing a heavy wooden chair towards the shelf. I threw myself bodily at the legs of the chair, bruising my panting chest and moving the chair by millimetres rather than centimetres at a time. Eventually I gave up and sat disconsolate in the middle of the room. I was alone. Alone with my aching ribs and the warmth of my self-pity which welled up inside, breaking every resistance, and bringing tears to my eyes, and with it a kind of comfort. I could stand the solitude no longer and began to howl. The anguished animal scream came from the very depths of my puny body – the power that the weak can find in the hidden reserves of their despair.

It may have been very loud indeed, because in no time I heard human voices and running on the stairs. The bald Bacchus stamped into the room, followed by a companion. 'How the hell did that get in here?' he cried and at the same time grabbed me and threw me bodily down the first flight of stairs. 'Where's Fotis? Off on one of her jaunts? Throw that animal out.'

I collected my battered frame and ran ahead, chased by Bacchus' soulless voice, which came closer each time I lost a second by tripping on the stairs, until on the last flight, nearing a large mirror in a well-light hall, I saw myself. I had become that absurd creature designed to be pampered by those who have a deep-seated need to pamper. I had become a poodle.

* * * * *

Captatio benevolentiae

So that, reader, is the story of my first metamorphosis. I feel perhaps a little self-conscious about addressing you with so familiar and so dated a term as 'reader'. By calling you this name, I intrude upon your activity, I draw attention to the very artificiality of your pastime, you strange, loveable, abstract and amorphous companion of my tale. Stay with me! Be generous and suspend your disbelief. Let me capture your benevolence and take it for a walk.

Little can be achieved by regret: Fotis was ultimately to be my saviour, and I had at least learnt not to trust anyone who offers to point out the point to it all, not because there isn't necessarily a point: it is just rather unlikely that anyone will ever discover what it is. Those Bacchus-worshippers thought it was pleasure. Fair enough, perhaps a better try than most. But if you pursue a particular purpose, it will fly off like a frightened bird. You bear it no harm, you merely wish to approach as near as you can, but perversely it misinterprets your desires and rushes into a trap left by others who do not hold it in such esteem. Better to study it from afar. Perhaps that is why the Epicureans lived like monks, in spite of their belief in pleasure and the mortality of the soul. 'Press the button for pleasure' is the modern religion, press the button to avoid boredom and silence, which hover like medieval demons. And silence is no longer allowed.

Those people took me away, and though I did not know it then, I was never to return to my Croydon home, to my grey-suited salesman father who must have hidden something behind so much conformity, to my perfect and sure-footed sister who appeared to hide nothing and perhaps nothingness beneath her well-ordered life. My mother had hidden herself by death, my father was shortly to follow her, and though I did meet my sister much later in life, after her divorce, and to our mutual delight, she was so changed that I could hardly believe that she was in fact the same person.

They were taking me away to a life of great difficulties, of things that can be little understood, of unnatural physical changes, of bitter anguish and unreasonable hopes ... A life like any other, in fact. Look at any newborn baby, and then look at any very old man or woman. Are these the same species, the same kind of being? Alright, they've got the same number of limbs and basic shape, but how can they compare? Is there perhaps more in common between every newborn living thing than there is between a baby human and an old, breathless, wrinkled, arthritic burden of flesh and brittle bones? The one is all possibilities, no past and barely a present that goes beyond basic physical needs; the other is an intricate and possibly noble mantle of things past, things that cannot be changed but can be regretted, things that were forced upon their bearer and things that were grasped, things that fade like the translucent skin of those who have for long avoided death. My metamorphoses were to be more dramatic, but perhaps no more absurd or puzzling than these.

CHAPTER TWO

A Dog's Life

The author is almost killed by kindness and learns not to trust anyone who professes to love him.

Grave glares on fur-enfolded shoulders,
stare in the void of Oxford Circus,
moulded in moisturising cream and powders,
they barely touch the movement of my mind,
move solidly on solid principles,
well-husbanded with the professional kind.
Ladies, your chirling chins sag in waxing waves of fat,
kissed by lips chilled and habit entwined.

AS I MADE MY way through the night, perceiving its reality from the changed perspective of a viewpoint barely a foot off the ground, I was on my way to find my owner. At that time I wasn't aware of it, but simply being a dog in a western city entitles you to the very best of homes, while mere human beings are left to freeze, sleeping rough in the parks, railway stations and under bridges. At first light as I dragged my bedraggled body aimlessly along, an official appeared from an organisation dedicated to the welfare of stray dogs. I was taken to some kennels in the country in his van where I was fed, scrubbed and put in a cage. After a few days a lady wearing the fur of some less cherished and less protected species appeared and made approving noises around my cage. From there I was taken to a mock-Tudor mansion on the outskirts of the city.

The owner of this luxurious abode ('three large reception rooms, six bedrooms, kitchen, pantry, twin garages, ample lawns, delightful view of the park, etc.') was Sir William Ambrose Plooter. He was a man of great substance, both in his person and in the goods and chattels that society and the wisdom of its laws recognised as exclusively his, although it must be said that he had only the vaguest of ideas as to where most of them were to be found and had to employ several people just to keep track of them. He worked hard, not because it gave him great pleasure but because he could earn such vast sums per hour, indeed per minute, that it seemed a terrible waste ever to sit down and relax. I therefore saw little of Sir William during my six-week sojourn in his home; it was his wife, Lady Thelma Plooter, who was to be my constant companion or owner.

Now, the poodle is a ridiculous animal and so it is natural that it should have ridiculous owners. Why should the similarity between pets and their owners surprise us? It is only natural that this affinity is greater than that between children and their parents, given that pets are chosen while children spring from some unfathomable genetic equation. Thelma had me washed and scrubbed endlessly, then she would have me combed under her supervision and then she would personally spray me with some perfume that smelt disgusting to my doggy nose. At the end of this, I felt like a canine gigolo, as overdressed as a dog can be in its nakedness. Indeed she sometimes inflicted the indignity of attaching red ribbons to my collar and tail. To be fair to Thelma, she was no kinder to herself. She spent hours wallowing in the bath, being massaged, having her hair done by a hairdresser who came to the house, applying large quantities of make-up so as to cover up her somewhat jowly features with an even more unpleasant mask, and covering herself with yet more of that expensive *parfum*.

These masochistic tendencies probably arose from her undoubted frustration with life in the mock-Tudor mansion. She had exactly the opposite problem to her husband: her time was worthless and dedicated to the unequal task of consuming some part of the immense fortune continually being coined by the time of Sir William. Her time fought his. She had to move slowly and think even slower. The business of using up the twenty-four hours the earth so sluggishly takes to simply turn around was made even more difficult for her by the fact that so many of the daily chores we take for granted were, in her case, performed by hired staff. Her clothes were ironed for her, her hair was brushed for her, her mask was applied to her face by skilled hands, saccharine was put in her coffee for her and then stirred, her car was driven for her and she never put her coat on herself as merely by approaching the front door, she set in motion the well-practised employees, so she would find her coat hanging from the two hands of a human coat-rack and stretched solicitously towards her. In short, she was left to perform only a few highly personal functions which her dignity found incompatible with the presence of others, such as wiping her arse, brushing her teeth, cleaning the inside of her nose with her little finger, weighing herself and waking up in the morning.

There was however one activity that Thelma was allowed by inclination and by decorum to engage in. It gave a purpose to all the endless preparations she inflicted on herself every day. It was of course charity work, that ancient solace to all rich women. Lesser intellects, such as my feeble doggy one, would have considered it much easier to have given some part of Sir William's immense fortune to the poor and needy, thus making them slightly less poor and needy, and at the same time releasing the unfortunate Sir William from his anxieties over a fortune that increased exponentially. But this is because we simple folk have confused charity with charity work. The purpose of the latter is to entertain and use up the time of the idle rich who are usually the wives, sons or daughters of some grafting and tenaciously mean money-making man with the touch of Midas. If these activities incidentally produce some small sums for charitable purposes, that is only to be commended, but it is considered bad taste to turn these small sums into large sums as this would introduce a disagreeable element of competition. Naturally Lady Thelma and her friends would never dream of voting for any party that wished to alleviate the causes of charitable concern by direct government intervention as this would threaten the very basis of their only pastime. Indeed Thelma was one of those enlightened people who considered it immoral to interfere in the plight of human beings – tantamount to meddling with the natural and presumably divinely ordained order of human society. On the other hand she didn't mind interfering with the natural order of nature and when it came to quadrupeds she believed in universal love and equality. Thus she lent the prestige of her name to many good causes that protected various species from the hedgehog to the dark-spotted lemur. Amongst her other onerous duties, she was chairwoman of the charity that had saved me from a life of canine vagrancy the night of my first metamorphosis.

Lady Thelma had an instinctive dislike for coffee mornings, an extremely lower-middle class institution, typical of the vulgar energy to be found amongst the wives of successful shopkeepers and the like. But when it came to charity teas, she was the past mistress of the genre. And it was to these that she and I dedicated our days, for I was obliged to share in her passion for post-meridian refreshment. The day after my arrival in Sir William's mock mansion, I made my debut in polite society. I was from the first a great success and Thelma was very proud of me. 'What a sweet little poodle! Where *did* you find him?' was a fairly typical sample of the far-from-varied conversation that my presence engendered, through an atmosphere so sticky with expensive perfume that the air could have had its contents distilled and sold on at a considerable profit. On our way home, my owner picked me up lovingly, and, caressing me, whispered sweet banalities into my ear that I am too embarrassed to repeat. Even a diminutive doggy has some dignity and I was beginning to regret the moment I had met my charitable saviours. It is true that I was well-fed, nor could I complain about my basketwork bed, and my only duties were to display myself to an admiring public. But I had this oppressive sensation of being owned, of being an object which my owner could dispose of in whatever way her fancy took her.

Thelma continued to squander her loving attentions on my furry form, to indulge her desire to pamper, perhaps sadly reflecting a desire to be pampered which had long been ignored in all but a pecuniary sense by the industrious Sir William. She called me Bobbles, appropriate enough for a small, curly and woolly object. It made me think of bauble. It must also be said that initially I had great status and was treated with almost reverence by all the members of the household. On the third evening I decided to test the limits of my powers and when Sir William came back from his long hard day at the office, I made straight for his favourite armchair and, making myself as comfortable as I could, pretended to be asleep. When the captain of industry found his chair occupied, he was uncertain as to what he should do and looked enquiringly at his wife for advice. 'You're not going to wake poor Bobbles, are you? Poor little dear, he's had a very long day. I took him to the Canine Conservation Committee's bring-and-buy sale this afternoon – he was such a darling. There are plenty of other chairs to sit on' she replied. Snorting, the financial wizard chose another chair, while I reflected on the paradoxical nature of property. A person can own and control vast wealth that he has never seen, but still not be in full control of his most immediate and intimate possessions, such as his own armchair.

However, my influence with the mock-Tudor monarch was short-lived: she soon began to tire of me, although not as quickly as I tired of her. Perhaps she sensed my doggish resentment, although she could never have guessed that I understood every word she said, and she spoke to me often.

She opened her heart to me and I was her supposedly deaf confessor. 'Bobbles, darling, I don't know what to do in town today. Shall we go shopping? Is that what little Bobbles would like to do? I'll get a little something for you too. That's right, you lucky thing. Now give Mummy a kiss'. At which point, I stared in terrified silence at her red lips. Where had they been, and how many quadrupeds had they kissed before me?

Sometimes her ramblings were pathetic: 'Bobbles darling, if it wasn't for you, I would be so lonely. Yes, Mummy would be lonely without her Bobbles,' and then more to herself: 'When is William going to get home? Does the little shit think I don't know what he's up to? Men!'

Sometimes she was just incomprehensible: 'I wish, Bobbles ... yes sometimes I just wish ... but then things never change. So bloody what! Maybe I'll do it anyway, just for the hell of it. Nobody's going to find out, are they, Bobbles? ... That would show them anyway. Oh yes, he'll regret it in the end.' These segments of thoughts were by far the most interesting things that Thelma ever said. I could expand on their possibilities, speculate on their meanings, and attribute them with a grandeur they probably didn't deserve. If you are owned, you must be concerned with your owner's feelings, because your own depend on them.

I had no idea how I was to escape from her overindulgent dominance, but I thought about it constantly. I dreamt of a life of adventure, tramping the streets and taking to the hills and byways. Always on the move. You could let the decades slip by in such dreams, but as it happened, things came to a head very quickly. Thelma had arranged a splendid cocktail party for Sir William's friends or, more precisely, business colleagues. She told me to be on my best behaviour and I decided that this would be the best opportunity not to follow orders and get myself returned to the peaceful cage in the kennels that she had taken me from. There was another reason for hoping that she might prefer my absence to my presence, and that was the arrival of an Afghan bitch (purely a reference to the number of this dog's chromosomes and no aspersion on her character). Now it has to be said that I have always been attracted to tall women, perhaps because in my human form I was considered tall, and my Afghan companion immediately aroused my doggy instincts.

The guests arrived, the Afghan hound and myself were circulating freely and I decided to initiate my antisocial behaviour. It is very difficult to make sexual advances in the standing position if the object of your desire is over twice your height, but my principle object was to assert my individuality by shocking the gathering and thereby embarrassing Thelma before her buzzing guest-swarm. I rose up on my back paws, a posture to which I was well-practised by my human past, displayed my red organ to all around and then tottered forward until I could place my front paws on the haunches of the Afghan lady. Her only reaction to my inopportune advances was to take one step forward, whereupon I fell flat on the floor. Her contemptuous indifference riled me and I attempted several more times to the same effect. Nor did my activity cause much of a stir. There were, it is true, a few titters, but my behaviour wasn't considered abnormal given that an animal has no control over its instincts, nor can it be expected to have a sense of social propriety. Disconcerted, I made my way to a corner of the room to think out a new plan. Clearly, if I wanted to shock, I had to do something that was unquestionably un-canine. Propriety is based on expectations within a given context; I simply had to find a way of breaking those rules.

Through a gap in the crowd came, like an inspiration, the vision of five layers of cream gateau, built like tower, a monument to gastronomic extremism. In a second I knew what I had to do. I raced through the gap, leapt onto the table and proceeded to eat the cake. The reaction was immediate: 'Hey look, that dog is eating cake', 'Can you believe it, a dog eating cake', 'Trust Thelma to feed her dog cake', 'Thelma, Thelma, how did you train your dog to do this?' Thelma, however, was not amused when my antics were pointed out to her. She had no desire to have the only cake-eating dog in the country, she abhorred the slightest deviance from the expected, and she would define such deviance universally as perversity. 'Bobbles, stop that at once! Get down from there, you disgusting dog!' Thelma's reaction only added to her guests' hilarity and her embarrassment. Just as she was about to get hold of me, I jumped away and bounded towards the drinks table. There was an open bottle of curaçao which I grabbed by my front paws as I rolled over onto my back, spilling much of the liquid as I went; with my back legs I raised the base of the bottle upwards so that the sticky liquid could pour into my mouth. I must admit that I had hardly predicted the reaction of the guests: far from being shocked, they began to applaud. 'The dog's a genius', 'Sir William's parties were never like this', 'How can he do that?'

This time I allowed Thelma to catch me. I considered that I had had the desired effect and it was probably not politic to anger her further. She grabbed me by the collar, and while the spectators interceded strongly on my behalf, she carried me to the bathroom, threw me inside and locked the door. My head was swimming partly as a result of being hurled against the side of the bath, and partly because of the sticky liquid, far too strong for my shrunken doggy brain. But in spite of my physical and mental battering, and indeed the awareness that I would feel even worse the following day, I enjoyed a quiet sense of achievement.

Victory, however, was to turn to disaster when in the morning I was woken and taken from my solitary confinement. Sure enough, my head ached and my body was bruised, but as I was put in the car I felt sure that I was returning to my cage, to a more conventional and congenial form of imprisonment (as far as imprisonment can ever be congenial, but it awaited me like paradise in that particular moment, because freedom is always a relative state of being). However, the destination turned out to be that of Thelma's veterinary surgeon. I was held in the waiting room by the chauffeur, while she had a long talk in the surgery.

Eventually I was taken in and placed on a table in the middle of the room while a fat man in a white coat was working away in the corner with his back towards me. Then he turned, pointed a syringe to the light and squeezed the plunger until a droplet of pinkish liquid appeared at the end of the needle; he then came towards me with a determined expression. I realised I had to act. My canine instinct was to leap at him, bite him, scratch him and then in the ensuing confusion make my escape. But my human reason told me that such behaviour would only strengthen his resolve and that my only hope was to placate him with words. 'Doctor,' I said, for I considered a formal and perhaps even servile approach was in order. 'Doctor, it has often occurred to me that the expression "put a dog to sleep" is a most cruel euphemism. I would never want to question any of your professional decisions, but I do feel that my former owner may have been imprecise in her account of the events that led to my appearance in your clinic.' I paused as the poor man backed off and sat down opposite, returning my stare with one of bewilderment.

'A dog that speaks!' he said, directing his words at nobody, for who would ever talk to a dog that can talk back. 'A dog that speaks is absurd. This cannot be happening.'

'I realise that it must be disconcerting to find yourself tête-à-tête with a dog, a poodle at that,' I returned, continuing my conciliatory tone, 'but we must face up to our problem. To inject me with that filthy liquid would be tantamount to murder, given that you would be killing a thinking and articulate being. On the other hand you don't want to get into trouble with Lady Thelma. I give you my solemn oath that if you release me through the back door, I will never show myself in this area again. Lady Thelma will never know that you didn't carry out her cruel orders.'

The vet looked at me distrustfully and then continued his reverie: 'Clearly dogs don't speak, so this must be some kind of mental aberration. I have put so many dogs to sleep that an innate sense of guilt is causing me to hallucinate.'

'Let me put your mind at rest on that score. I am a dog, but I used to be a human being and I have retained my powers of thought and speech. You see before you this doggy form, the meagre sinews of my meagre appetites, the incontinent slave of canine instincts. I pee up against walls and smell the arses of passing fellows of the species. I bark at old ladies and small children, and then I fawn and flatter whoever brings me food. But there is also a human soul in me and the proof is that I rebelled against the luxurious dictatorship of Lady Thelma; I stood up for my dignity even if by so doing I was certain to curtail considerably my standard of living. But never did I expect a death sentence. Indeed, had I known the risks, I may well have put my principles to one side and continued to suffer the suffocation of Lady Thelma's fickle attentions. You mustn't take me for what I appear but for what I say and plead before you – for you are my judge, jury and executioner.'

The vet continued to stare and to mutter his incredulity to himself. My words had had little effect on him and he seemed to refute their reality. I decided that to perorate may have only increased the obvious communication gap. I changed tactic and told a simple story in the hope of finally convincing him of my unusual predicament.

'There was once a fisherman, a poor fisherman is the usual expression in these stories, in any case a man much poorer than those who did not have to work for their living. One day a storm blew up and drove his boat onto some rocks where it soon broke up. The fisherman barely escaped with his life. Fear had given him the energy to swim to the beach, but once he reached its safety, fear gave way to exhaustion and despair. Not only had his livelihood been destroyed along with the boat, but he had no idea where he had landed or in which direction he had to go to return home on foot. After sleeping a few hours on the beach, he moved inland through a dense wood hoping to find a settlement where he could be better informed as to his whereabouts. Partly because of the difficulty of moving across such a terrain in a straight line and partly because the wood covered a wide territory all belonging to a powerful judge and confidant to the king, the fisherman walked for a day without meeting anyone. He decided to stop and with some string to set a few snares. When he returned from a search for wild fruits, he found that a rabbit had been caught in one of his snares. He was just about to cut the animal's throat when some gamekeepers arrived and dragged him off to the judge's house.

'The judge was a severe man and dealt harshly with poachers. In this case he felt particularly ill-disposed because the culprit had been found on his land, stealing his rabbit. When the fisherman was brought before the judge, he would have done well to have assumed a deferential attitude, but, convinced of his innocence, he decided to retain his dignity and plead the exceptional circumstances of the case. "My Lord, it would appear that you have before you a petty criminal caught red-handed in the act of stealing your property, but inside that outer appearance is an honest working man who maintains his family and in his small way contributes to the wealth of the state, to the apparatus of which you hold such an important and well-rewarded part. You must consider how I came to find myself on your land. I didn't come to it with the intent to steal, but was driven to it by the cruel connivance of wind and sea. Fate landed me on these shores and I was alone with the land. I couldn't know whose land it was or if it belonged to anyone at all. My natural appetites, my obvious human needs forced me to an act that has all the outward aspects of a crime but was in reality the only means of survival. Surely we all have a duty and a right to ensure the continuance of our own lives?" "Not at the expense of other people's property," replied the judge and found him guilty.

'The next day as the judge rode into town to sentence the guilty, he was stopped by an old woman. "My lord," she said, "I must speak with you of the fisherman that you must sentence today. His son is to be a great warrior, a captain of soldiers, a destroyer of cities and a maker of kings. If you condemn the fisherman to death, not only will you commit an injustice but his family will flee abroad and the military skills of the son could be turned against your state instead of becoming its willing instrument." The judge reacted with disdain and spurred his horse. How could the son of a mere fisherman become a great general? But as he rode, the old woman's words began to unsettle him, because they exposed the fragility of the state, the flux of national borders, and the precariousness of wealth. In his career he had ignored military affairs which he considered better dealt with by the uncouth. Violence was the affair of the populace and only violence could keep them in place. Occasionally, however, unruly elements who excelled in the matter of arms would appear and usurp the right to organise terror; armies would grow like mushrooms, descend from the woods and shake even well-ordered civilisations. Prophesy is insidious, self-creating, pleading to be believed because of its absurd pretensions. The woman was probably mad but if she was right, he could avoid disaster simply by releasing the fisherman, which would have cost him nothing except his reputation for severity. He decided to be prudent and take the woman's advice.

'When however the culprit appeared before him with an impudent expression of innocence, the judge's nature had its way, anger rose up and he scorned his lack of virility and superstitious fears. To release such a man would have been to encourage every insolent villain to help himself to all the animals of his forest. He sentenced the fisherman to be hanged the next morning.

'The years passed and one day the king summoned the judge to his court where he was told that the neighbouring country, although much smaller, had amassed a mighty army largely made up of discontents from the wilder and mountainous regions of both countries. They were commanded by a warlord, a savage captain who captured his men's hearts with rebellious words of past injustices and plunder to be had. The neighbouring country was sending him more in the hope that his unruly regiments would be cut to pieces than that territory would be acquired by so unpredictable a servant of their state. But there was little chance of inflicting such a defeat and the king thought it best for the judge to go to the enemy camp and plead with the general to change sides. He should be offered a dukedom, large sums of money, and it was even possible to appeal to his patriotism as he apparently originated from their own nation, from a fisherman's family. The judge immediately remembered the old lady's prophecy and realised that a prophecy that had proved true in part was likely to be proved true in all its parts. However, he had little choice but to follow his king's command and go to the enemy camp.

'To his horror the general recognised him immediately as his father's killer and when asked how this was possible the general replied that an old lady had told him that he would one day be a mighty warlord and that when in vengeance he moved against his own country, he would be met by the very man who had so cruelly and unjustly condemned his father to death. "You see these men," he said pointing to the coarse ruffians that surrounded him, "they represent the accumulated injustices of your fine cities and wealthy gentry. Men who have been beaten for stealing bread made from the corn that they had grown themselves. Men who preferred the dangerous and harsh existence in the mountains to the stench of servility in the well-ordered arrogance of your hierarchy, your chains of command, and ladders of insincerity and ambition. These are men who frighten you because they fear death less than slavery." "But what are you going to do with me?" asked the quaking judge and the general replied: "I always thought that I would only find you some extremely uncomfortable prison, because the old lady also told me that if I were to give full rein to my vengeance and hang you as you did my father,

I would overreach myself and within a year I would be poisoned by an ally, a treacherous king, and the old order would re-establish itself as firmly as before. But now I see you shivering before me, I feel such disgust that I can only follow my nature and hang you from the nearest tree." Within the hour, the judge's considerable bulk weighed from the branch of a tree and the defiant captain rode out to do battle against an army and against a prophecy.'

The vet continued to stare in disbelief and I waited to see the effect of my words, believing it inevitable that his imagination would make that leap between his situation and that of the judge. But the more I thought about it, the more it occurred to me that the meaning of the story was not that executioners should learn to show clemency, but rather that they will always carry out their professional task, whatever the risk. I must have miscalculated either the pride he took in his work or his fear of Lady Thelma, for murder returned to his eyes and he stood up brandishing the syringe. My life flashed before me, both human and canine, I was on the point of being butchered for having acted badly at a party. The punishment was totally disproportionate to the crime, but there was no way of talking to this man. I made recourse to oldest of tricks, practised in every playground in the country. I yelled: 'Look out behind you, quack!' and as he instinctively turned, he gave me just enough time to make my escape across the room and through a half-open window. Life and liberty were there, if my little legs would move fast enough. In spite of being horribly overweight and unfit, my pampered limbs, driven by adrenaline, rose to the occasion, and I was at the window in a moment. The air that came through the window was sweet with the scent of the garden, contrasting with the disinfectants and other disagreeable smells of the animal surgery. How we love the things we believe we are to be deprived of! The newly cut lawn with its neat rows of contrasting greens beckoned, and then it all disappeared in a flash of shock and pain.

The man, probably no fitter than I, had also found unsuspected physical resources, urged not by fear but an insane desire to impose that merciless will that, I have observed, appears to abide in the hearts of some men. After a few skips, he had also nearly reached the window, and, stretching out a powerful hand, had grasped me most rudely by the hairs on my rear quarters, and swung me back on to the operating table without regard to the items of furniture that I met with along the way.

'Let me go you lump of lard – you loathsome piece of shit,' I said, having decided that politeness and diplomacy now served no useful purpose. Have you ever reflected, reader, on the perverse nature of human beings? How so much of our discourse is driven by what we and others expect of ourselves. How social context, accent and dress govern our speech and behaviour. Our veterinary surgeon, who had refused to enter into direct conversation with me because I was wearing my furry canine suit, now entered into fierce exchange of epithets that did not recognise the boundaries of species. 'Keep still, you four-legged loud-mouthed lout of a dog from hell. You shit-head! If you try and bite my fingers once more, I'll break your bleeding neck.'

Many more insults he heaped upon me, and many I returned in kind. Down came the needle and pierced my thigh, and my poor doggy frame shuddered. I prepared to meet my maker, in my base and pathetic form. My lust for Fotis and my lust for the Afghan lady had landed me in this predicament. I was to die without knowing a little of my humanity. A dog.

At that moment, the door swung open and in came a woman, also dressed in a white coat, and also corpulent and irascible. 'What the hell is going on? Who are you swearing at? Don't you know that all the customers can hear you? Who were you talking to, anyway?'

'I was talking to the dog, you stupid bitch. Can't you see I was talking to the dog.'

'I see, you were talking to the dog,' said the woman, stressing and slowing down the pronunciation of the last two words. 'Do you do this often?'

'The dog was talking to me, you stupid cow. The bloody dog was talking to me.'

Let me stop here to explain that these two were both colleagues, and man and wife. Professional rivalries were heaped upon the bickering intolerance that is to be found in many marriages. Theirs was a relationship that rarely rose above a tiresome exchange of the mutual desire to humiliate the other. People can become quite dependent on such relationships – often the most long-lasting unions.

'Have you finally gone mad? Are you trying to tell me that that dog was talking to you? Are you hallucinating?'

'I tell you the dog was talking to me. Weren't you, doggy?' he added pleadingly to me. A syringe full of lethal liquid stuck into your thigh concentrates the mind admirably. It occurred to me that the man would not want to push down the plunger and propel me into some doggy afterlife until I spoke to the woman and thus re-established his sanity. It also occurred to me that by remaining silent or only emitting canine sounds, I stood a good chance of lengthening my life expectancy.

The man pleaded with me and the woman upbraided him at each desperate attempt. He removed the syringe, still containing its fatal dose, and started to talk to the woman, half pleading for her to believe him and half warning her that if she didn't, she would pay for it. He waved the syringe in front of her.

'Are you threatening me with that thing?'

'Yes,' he cried, 'yes, I am,' and with another demonstration of alacrity, he thrust the syringe into her ample backside and pushed the plunger in as far as it could go. I doubt the dose was lethal to a human being, but in any case she did not seem to take much notice. By way of reply, she lifted up a large veterinary tome and brought it down on his skull with a crack that made me wince.

The time had come, I felt, to make good my escape. Slightly limping from my sore thigh, I silently reached the open window and slithered through without their noticing. I do not know and I little care how that battle of the titans ended. Blow was followed by blow, and neither seemed to get the upper hand. The powerful can shake the heavens, and the weak just get on with their lives. I left them to their conjugal combat, and crossed the geometric tidiness of the garden and slipped out of their lives forever.

Once I was safe, I realised that top priority had to be finding the fake church and getting myself turned back into a human being, given that a dog's life had turned out to be pretty hazardous. The finding was the difficult part, but after two days on the run, avoiding charitable officials and curious children, I climbed through a window above a dustbin and made my way up those fateful stairs. Once in the room, I was again faced with the problem of which ointment to use and how to reach them. I then discovered a jar in the corner covered with dust and hairs. Given that it was my only chance I took a pawful and attempted to rub it onto my body. Again there was searing pain and again I felt my limbs contracting still more. My hair turned bright colours. It was clear that I wasn't turning back into my former self.

CHAPTER THREE

Speech Without Thought

The author takes on a feathered form, is carefully looked after by someone who perceives him as merchandise, and then neglected by someone who means well. He listens to male humour, and experiences male callousness.

I often well-evaded words will search
in searching to affirm myself,
the little man, whose longed-for line
would time encase, and parcel up
those joys, that each the meagre twine
as yet uncut will allocate, and which
the sullen Parchae interlace
with coarser threads, those golden darts.
And then the cut;
the stuff is trussed and wound around;
atom-tight, the fading ball is placed upon the stack.
Who will consume and thus unthread this fast-decaying
  matter of the past,
and who will read the latent phonemes
punched within the solid moulds and cast
within the rigid rhythms of my mind?

A PARROT'S FLIGHT is dissimilar to that of the eagle in almost every respect. I had to beat my wings continually, having almost no gliding ability, and still I seemed to fall. I guided my graceless passage towards a rooftop. Once I had made my clumsy landing, I stood panting, desperately trying to fill those tiny lungs; my claws grasped the rounded edge of a tile as the wind buffeted my feeble frame. Even as I tried to catch my breath, my mind was overcome by my predicament and each problem seemed more intractable than the other. I was of course starving, and I hadn't the strength to return to the church tower. Outside, my battered body would have few chances of survival. The obvious thing was to fly to the nearest pet shop and give myself up as it were. That way I would solve all my most pressing survival problems, but I would also run the risk of remaining a parrot for the rest of my natural life. Some stones thrown by a group of passing schoolchildren convinced me that survival was the priority – I would plan my escape once my strength had returned. In any case, the chances of finding the correct ointment to undo my metamorphoses appeared to be slim.

I staggered breathless into a shop in the high street that I had often passed in the capacity of potential client rather than voluntary merchandise. On entering, in grave danger of being stamped on by one of the clients, I found myself in that repulsive environment that to anyone else smells of animals and animal foods, but to me in that particular moment smelt of safety and an honest home. 'Where did that bird come from? I didn't know parrots migrated this far north,' said the bewildered shopkeeper. To say that the cage that he put me in seemed like a room in the Savoy would probably be an exaggeration: the simile certainly wouldn't be based on any personal experience. I suppose a more realistic comparison to describe the sense of comfort I found there, would be to say it was like a well-cleaned motel bedroom, Spartan but sufficient. There was food and drink, and as birds have the absurd habit of sleeping standing up, one perch is very much like another.

For several weeks I was incarcerated in the pet shop, quite happy with the daily routine. A safe, regular and near affluent lifestyle. I had little to complain of as everything was done to ensure that I became a healthy and therefore more saleable specimen. Institutions can give a sense of security that for some outweighs the oppression of monotony. If somebody is concerned about your well-being, it is in a way quite flattering. We are blind to the ulterior motives. We want so much to be loved: the weaker we are, the greater that desire and the more likely we are to believe in the goodness of our benefactors. I really felt the shopkeeper treasured me for my unique colouring and for the originality of the manner in which I became part of his stock. We treasure the great from our position of mediocrity, and we despair when they finally betray us.

Of course, we often have these periods in our lives, in which we feel so secure that we are hardly aware of how empty our existence is. After all, my position was not as undignified and disagreeable as that of Bobbles the poodle. We forget how much we are controlled by those who control us, like our superiors at work or in society, and it takes a sudden event to make us realise the true state of affairs.

One day, while I was snoozing happily on my perch, I suddenly found that the cage was in motion. It changed hands and I changed property, the pet-shop owner, bless his kind heart, solicited on my behalf that the cage should be cleaned at least every two days. And in the same instant I was in the street, in a car and then hurtling towards my new home.

On reflection, I had every reason to be pleased with this turn of events, as I somehow felt that it would be easier to escape. Events had thrown me back on my own resources, I was a parrot alone. I waited with mixed feelings to be introduced to my new family. Three children crowded round straight away, and at the same time I was able to get a better look at their father who had bought me. He was a tall, thin, sickly individual with a protruding chin and sunken eyes. He attempted to communicate with his children in two very different but probably connected ways. Either he would speak to them pleadingly in an even-toned and meek voice or he would shout at them in a high-pitched shrill. Neither method proved particularly effective, and the man seemed from the beginning to be losing control of himself and his children. But it would appear that families can maintain these states of high tension for extended periods of time, a kind of inertia of misery.

'Does it talk?' the children cried, but I did not answer because I wanted to practise my parrot voice at night before I tried it out on them. 'It will do in time,' the father replied. The children clicked their tongues as though to say 'Trust dad to buy a stupid parrot that doesn't even know how to speak.'

Their father, it turned out, was a schoolteacher and his wife worked in the same profession. She lusted for power and prestige, and despaired at her husband's ineffectual nature. Driven by this oppressive demon, she would occasionally retire to bed exhausted with a headache, with ulcered anxiety that derived either from unachieved ambitions or from ambitions achieved whose achievement was delusory. She demanded authority and was given it, but not love, while he was grudgingly loved but little respected. There was a constant feeling that something was going to snap, but it never did. The children were always late for everything: screams, anxiety, tears, accusations. Everyone was grinding their teeth, hanging on.

A fine situation to find yourself in, as a caged parrot and captive audience. I had to watch this scene day in day out, and regretted leaving the benign monotony of the pet shop – I was weak amongst the weak, an equality of unhappiness. For the first month or so, the schoolteacher looked after me as I deserved, but then interest began to flag; some days I was given no food and my cage was cleaned at ever-increasing intervals. There was one advantage in being a parrot: nobody became hysterical when I spoke. Of course I had to limit myself to parrot-like statements, uttered with a suitably parrot-like accent. 'Good morning, Polly,' clearly raised no eyebrows. Nor did 'Roger!' which was the teacher's name and was often shouted around the house. Each new utterance renewed interest and supplies of food; I found that I had literally to sing for my supper, or more precisely to squawk for it. When I showed that I knew the name of every member of the household including the cat, they started to consider me a very special bird indeed. For a time I was pointed out to guests, who always revolutionised the family's behaviour. Indeed when guests stepped into the house, the family was hardly recognisable; politeness not only took over but went to exaggerated extremes. Sentences were clearly thought out and pronounced in subdued tones; concern and care for others were displayed convincingly. In short the family was made up of well-trained actors that put on a show for visiting audiences. And I became part of that show, at least for a while. They were to be envied because they owned such a clever bird. As their property, my glory was not mine but theirs. But when all their friends had seen me and tired of my repertoire, the family started to neglect me again.

When you're a parrot in a cage, you have little opportunity for dialogue. On the other hand you have ample opportunity to observe human dialogue, or what is often passed off for it. Five people can share a house and keep totally separate orbits, never stopping to communicate their feelings. My five cohabitants were all what might be defined as nice people, indeed their public image may have been more real than the private one. Roger was well-meaning but weak; Amelia, his wife, was wilful, intelligent but enfeebled by unrealised desires; the children were what children are in such situations, wild but secretly more mature than their argumentative parents. Their only fault was to share the same roof, because by so doing, Roger became feebler and Amelia, frustrated by his weakness and hers, more despotic. Each spoke as in a Pinter play, following the trajectory of their individual thoughts or speaking by rote in their ritualised relationships.

One evening the teacher was alone in the house, reading the newspaper in his armchair near my cage. I had had enough, so discarding my parroty pretence, I spoke directly to him: 'Didn't the man in the pet shop instruct you to clean my cage at least every two days? But here I am sitting in last week's shit. Pull yourself together you self-pitying wimp. Clean my cage and make yourself useful, instead of moping around and reading articles about things that have nothing to do with you.' Of course he might have just got up and wrung my frail neck, but I think I had correctly analysed his character and predicted his probable reactions. At first he couldn't understand where my voice was coming from, but then he just stared at me open-mouthed.

I let the shock work on him for a bit, and noticing no signs of aggression, I decided to go a great deal further. 'Look, I'm caged, but so are you. Let me give you some advice.'

'Why do you call me a wimp?' he said in an offended tone.

'I'll come to that,' I replied, 'but first let me explain that this is no hallucination. I have been transformed into parrot ...'

'By a wicked witch,' he suggested with a sarcastic sneer which implied he had already agreed to enter into a dialogue of equals, in spite of my parroty appearance.

'Not wicked, I believe. And the cause was my meddling with things I could not understand. It doesn't matter now. It is important that you believe me. My name is, or was, Lucian Hector Heatherington-Jones.'

'That is certainly a strange name for a parrot.'

'And for a human being. My father's neo-classical taste in forenames combined improbably and somewhat unhappily with I-know-not-what permutations that led to that particular double-barrel. As I am the only male offspring, you might say that I am the last of the Heatherington-Joneses.'

'And as you have now become a parrot, you could say that you are an endangered species ... So you've been spying on me ... on us. Why do you say that what goes on in the world has nothing to do with me?'

'Because your energies can hardly deal with your present misery.'

'That's a bit dramatic.'

'When misery becomes a habit, it is sometimes hard to recognise. It arises from your inability to be yourself.'

'I'm being psychoanalysed by a parrot! Isn't it possible to feel at a home with a certain kind of discontent and isn't a certain degree of unhappiness inevitable?'

'You may be right. It isn't happiness you're missing out on, it's existence. Human existence only distinguishes itself from lower forms of life, if its abilities are stretched to their limit. You have to find your self and then push that self to its limit of existence.'

'Sounds highly suspect. It sounds like the philosophy of a yuppie or a sergeant-major.'

'No, you misunderstand me. I'm not talking about discipline imposed by others or by ambition, I'm talking about ...'

'Not self-discipline. Do you think a teacher hasn't heard that one. That's our stock-in-trade. If you want to be my shrink, Parrot, you will have to be a little more original. Your philosophy of activism tires me just to listen to it. It was invented by selfish academics who knew nothing of life's complexities, of responsibilities, of ... Why am I talking like this to you, a parrot? Why am I sitting here talking to a parrot?'

'You're quite right. It is not my place to judge or to advise you, and most un-parrotlike of me. I will promise to be more of a parrot, if you promise to be less of one with your wife and children. I tell you what,' I added in a confidential tone, 'take me to the pub on your shoulder, Long-John-Silver-style. I promise to be good if you will let me slurp from a half-pint of bitter.'

Outside, the night air ruffled my coloured feathers and infused me with an invigorating sense of freedom. Freedom, like so many things, is a relative state, and the pleasure of it is to be felt when it suddenly increases. Presently we arrived at the Brewers' Arms, a delightful little tavern, tastefully decorated with wall-to-wall fruit-machines and festooned with well-Brassoed horse-brasses, a temple to the unmannered manners of the English art of drinking. Since ancient times we have searched the solace of the tavern door, the haven of well-fermented liquor that swims within the mind and whose specific gravity is to lighten the gravity of our thoughts. Our civilisation has swelled upon this yeast, this catalyst of our desires and thoughts. If it weren't for beer halls and bars, we would be in the hands of fanatics, the tight-lipped, ashen-faced ayatollahs, the tight-collared, dog-collared priests who soft-smiling hide in honeyed words the reproving sneers of their blind faith. But we are grist to their mill, we are the source of their sense of virtue, the untiring superiority of their certainties. It is good to let the pious feel pious; they have no other use or purpose.

But what of the synthetic atmosphere of the Brewers' Arms, stamped like a plastic toy in the same mould as a hundred thousand other bars? The publican was cordial enough and greeted Roger as the prodigal son: 'Does the missus know you're out?' and 'Where did you get that parrot from?' My presence caused much amusement, especially when Roger presented me with the promised half of bitter. Several of the company commented on the schoolteacher's long absence from the Brewers' Arms and the severity of his wife. Perhaps it was this theme that suggested the tale that was told by a man with a neatly-trimmed moustache, wearing a Bavarian hat, which is possibly worth repeating here:

'Once there was a schoolteacher, a sad man whose wife was a real shrew (no resemblance to present company is intended). The reason for his unhappiness was not the nagging ways of his spouse but absurdly it was the fear that she was unfaithful to him. He was tortured by jealousy and would find excuses to return home at odd hours to see if he could surprise her with her lover, catch her red-handed and red-faced. One day he sold their caravan that they had been trying to sell for several weeks. This was more than pretext enough to rush home and give the good news to his wife. As he returned she was just saying good-bye to her lover, a young and lusty lad, a student from the local polytechnic. When she heard the husband's car, she quickly hid him in the caravan. The husband spun his car into the drive, parked it and as he jumped out he cried "Dearest, you'll never guess what. I've just sold the caravan!" and all the time he looked around suspiciously and almost sniffed the air for the smell of adultery. "Quickly – we must clean it, before the buyer comes," he said as he rushed to open the caravan door. The quick-witted wife opened the door first and asked assertively: "How much did you get for it then?" "Sixteen hundred, not bad eh? Nearly the asking price". The student was listening to every word, shaking as he did so, because the schoolmaster's jealousy was legend and he was reputed to carry a flick-knife just for such eventualities. However, when he heard the wife's next reply he knew exactly what to do. She started to berate the husband: "Trust a sucker like you to give it away for a silly price. I have just sold it for nineteen hundred; the buyer is having a look over it at this very moment." At this point the student came out, testing the hinges on the door and tapping the side as though he was looking for damp. "Yes, yes, that's fine. I'll take it. How much did you say? Nineteen hundred pounds?" "That's right" "Okay, but you'll have to clean it inside though; the floor and furniture are filthy." The husband at this point had forgotten all about his suspicions, transfixed, as it were, by the nineteen hundred pounds: "Let me do it!" and he ran to get a bucket and mop. As he set to work in the caravan, his wife stood on some boxes, leaned her head through one of the windows and started to give him instructions: "Come on, can't you see that mucky bit in the corner ... under the washbasin ... inside the cupboard". The student standing outside noticed how her splendid body bent forward and her buttocks moved as she stretched her arm and pointed first in one direction then in another. As he studied her litheness, he found desire for the activity that he had only recently been engaged in returning to his crotch. He looked round furtively and noticed how isolated the schoolmaster's house was, and so, after lowering his jeans and hers, he thrust at her as do the wild mustangs mating freely on the featureless and endless prairie and she, suppressing a cry both of humour and of joy at the risk they were running, continued to instruct the husband severely on how he should clean the caravan.'

'These stories are told parrot-fashion,' the teacher said quietly. 'They are simple, bawdy, meaningless and capable of surviving millennia. If it is true that marriage is breaking down as an institution, this kind of anti-uxorial joke could perhaps find itself in trouble.'

'Oh, *anti-uxorial*! Haven't we swallowed the dictionary? What's that supposed to mean?'

'Well, you know, that mindless tradition of jokes against wives – only next in popularity to those against mothers-in-law.'

'And what's wrong with a good mother-in-law joke. Have you heard this one?'

'Why anti-uxorial?' I whispered with my beak close to his ear. 'It is the husband who is the figure of ridicule. Besides, don't let your prudish principles spoil the cynical pleasure in the tale. It follows the logic of prankish humour; it requires the cunning deceiver and the fool. It has little to do with reality, with thought or with ideas; that's why it lasts. An element of cruelty must exist, because it has to portray a simple world motivated by the desire to do all others down. It is a world of Thatcherian competitiveness and disregard for others, mitigated by the innocence of the unscrupulousness described. It is a world that could never exist.'

'I understand. You sympathise with the fool, the butt of the joke, in this case the husband,' he returned. 'On the other hand, you admire the perpetrators of the prank, the sureness of their cunning which is untrammelled by any moral sense and therefore has a kind of innocence. You mentioned Thatcherian competitiveness, and objectionable as the essence of that "morality" may be, the truly repellent part is just that: its attempt to dress itself up as a morality. The amoral joke in a world that could never exist backs up an evil "morality" in the real world.'

'Well, I don't know about all that. Moral hypocrisy is not party political. But this humour does appeal to the law of the jungle.'

'But who is the real victim of the story?' he continued. 'Perhaps it isn't the foolish and jealous husband, who after all gets a good price for his caravan. Perhaps it's the student who has paid too much for goods he did not require.'

'Certainly,' I replied to my schoolteacher friend, 'or even the wife who must, for some unexplained reason, continue to share her life with a man she justifiably despises.'

'That's a splendid parrot you have there,' said one of the company staggering towards us, 'can it talk?'

'Roger! Roger!' I started to squawk obligingly and by way of a reply.

'So *it* nags you too!' joked the man looking sideways towards the proprietor. 'It has learnt who's boss, having lived in your house. Let's have a closer look.'

A large and sweating face loomed up before me, breathing alcoholic fumes from stubbled cheeks. 'Is that all he can say?'

I obliged again and began to sing in a parroty voice: 'What shall we do with the drunken sailor?'

'What's this? You've taught him sea shanties!' and the publican came over fascinated by my song. 'What else can he do?'

I had only been able to drink half of the half of bitter, and half of that I had splashed over the table, but even what I had drunk was a lot for my tiny parroty brain. I was beginning to enjoy my audience and, forgetting my promise to Roger, I began to go through a whole repertoire of songs that seemed suitable for my parroty self. They applauded me and congratulated my owner. First he took most of the credit, because they thought he must have worked very hard to have taught me those songs but soon they realised that I was no ordinary bird, but a genius amongst parrots. The words that came had no meaning for me and grasped from my memory purely at random; it was the effect they had upon my fellow tipplers that mattered: the joyous orgasm of surprise and each time I wanted to surprise them more. Little did I know how much danger I was putting myself in through my thoughtlessness, although my unfortunate owner, who wriggled his shoulder under my feet, was aware of the risk I was taking.

'How much for the bird?' demanded the publican who couldn't take his eyes off me.

'He's not for sale,' said Roger protectively.

'Come on, every man has his price. I could double my clientele with that animal – he would be a real attraction, a singing parrot. I'll give you a hundred quid and you can train yourself another one.'

Even in my alcoholic haze I found this bartering for my feathers somewhat distasteful.

'I'll give two hundred and that's my last offer.'

'I've told you that this bird is not for sale.'

The publican lost his patience and grabbed Roger by the collar: 'I'll pay you two hundred and fifty! And if you don't accept, I'll smash your bleeding face in!' The publican was not a man who was choosy about his words. Verbal originality was not a value that he held very highly and Roger, my friend and confidant, must have feared that he was as plain in his actions as he was in words, because he accepted the offer immediately. Prudence is the better part of valour, but in the meantime I had been sold into slavery – I had been delivered into the hands of violent men for lucre, betrayed for pieces of silver. Now I would be expected to entertain the punters with my songs. The publican counted out two hundred and fifty pounds and gave them to Roger, who folded up his principles in them and left the room without even taking a last guilty look at me. I was roughly placed in a cardboard box which had two breathing holes improvised in the top. If it hadn't been for my drunkenness and the lack of oxygen in that tiny box I would probably have been able to effect my escape that evening by tearing at the holes with my beak, thus saving myself from the mortal danger that I was to face once again.

When morning came, they brought a fine large cage and hung me in it over the bar, so all could see. When the bar opened at midday, I was unable and unwilling to sing. Unwilling because I was not particularly enamoured of the treatment I was receiving and unable because my head was being continually pounded by the most terrible hangover a parrot has ever experienced. As the afternoon wore on and it approached evening opening time, the publican became increasingly nervous and I could hear him muttering down below: 'Sing, damn you!'

It was then that I decided that if I were to be completely silent he might tire of keeping me in birdfood and restore my liberty to me. Of course, I was simply repeating my mistake with Thelma, but such is life: we rarely learn from past errors and seem destined to repeat them all our lives. When people own things, even living things, they expect them to do what is expected of them, or they dispose of them as they wish. As the evening wore on, his aggressive impatience came to the fore and he would punctuate the order, 'Sing, damn you!' which he now shouted, by banging the side of my cage with a piece of wood. But I showed great courage and stuck to my resolution, even when the cage swung violently, shuddering like a ship in trouble and giving me the sensation of seasickness. As you can well imagine, the events of that evening were discussed for many years by the regulars at the Brewers' Arms and gave rise to two expressions that have since passed into common usage: 'as sick as a parrot' and 'Who rattled your cage?' After a bit, the man in the Bavarian hat, who apparently propped up that bar every night, said 'Perhaps he needs something to drink. That guy last night gave him some beer before he began to sing.' The publican thought this a very good idea, and took the cage down, stood it on the bar and opened the cage door. I obligingly walked out and he placed in front of me a half of bitter, which I sipped twice to much applause. I was immediately planning my escape and walked up and down the bar waiting for the next customers to open the door.

When my opportunity came, I flew towards the door as fast as my puny wings could carry me, screeching loudly to make a passage through the crowd of drinkers, but I wasn't fast enough. The publican screamed to shut the door, and some public-spirited punter made a grab for me. All hell let loose as I veered away, the publican and a few others in hot pursuit. Tables were overturned and glasses spilt to screams of laughter at the grotesque comedy and of irritation at being soaked with some alcoholic beverage or other. Pandemonium – and for me alone it also held all its hellish associations. Finally I took refuge swinging on a lampshade and looking down upon the bobbing waves of bemused expressions, and feeling safe, I began to squawk as though taunting them and their lack of agility. What induced me to that folly, to that false sense of security? While I was fooling myself on my chances of survival, the publican, a tall and burly man, struck me from behind with his ever-present cudgel. I fell to the ground stunned, and my bruised body was then placed in the cage. The publican then offered to replace the spilt drinks and I was probably the topic of conversation for the rest of the evening, although I was too dazed to take any of it in.

My first plan worked up to a point, but again I had been unable to foresee that for most people 'getting rid' of an animal involved its physical annihilation. After the pub had closed and they had finished tidying up, the publican said to the lad that helped behind the bar: 'Seeing as that dumb bird has no intention of singing, I'm not going to pay for his supper. Take him out, pull his bleeding neck and toss him in the dustbin. Two hundred and fifty nicker up the spout and thirty more in free drinks!'

You can probably imagine how this statement concentrated the feeble powers of my limited bird-size grey matter. It looked as though I would have to forego all chance of ever having a Christian burial, but divine intervention was about to save me and events were just about to catch up with my executioner before he could execute his gruesome task. First let me tell you a little more about this unsavoury specimen of human thoughtlessness. He was one of those who finds a meaning for his meaningless existence by the certainty that his race is superior to all other races. Unfortunately individuals of this kind can be found in every 'race' (to use their terminology) which constitutes, I suppose, a kind of negative proof of our common humanity. This kind of superiority and intolerance is perhaps a genetic disorder that afflicts a small proportion of all populations to the detriment of all. It is an instinct that has to be obeyed, and once obeyed it searches for reasons to justify that sense of racial conceit. This lad was not familiar with the battles of Crecy or Agincourt, nor could he remember much about the Spinning Jenny or Stevenson's Rocket; he never grasped the reality of these gems of schoolroom jingoism but he accepted the general cultural climate that they seemed to confirm. Most of all he was aware that his country had once governed over many others, but that now it was reduced to an empire of rocks which it jealously protected against other countries keen to add a few rocks to their own territory. He suffered for his country's loss of power and status, as though it was a personal loss, as though his people had ever benefited from that power. And he felt, although he never asked himself why, that the enemy must have somehow cheated, or worse that his race had lost its historic purpose through some inexplicable process of corruption, presumably set in motion by the malevolent foreigner, incapable of accepting his subjugation in a spirit of civilised resignation. You may believe that he had at least a sense of human solidarity within the context of the nation, but this was not the case. He didn't like people from the north or for that matter from any of the other cardinal points. Even in his own county there were areas he didn't like. Then he didn't like people who were too posh or too common; he didn't like people who put on airs or people who didn't have standards; he didn't like those who try to cheat you or those who are suckers. In the end it turned out he was one of an extremely restricted number of the racially pure. His was an existence that on meeting another would think 'There goes a not-I' while a more generous soul would think 'There goes another I.'

But of course man is a social animal, and even such an unsociable individual has to seek out like-minded companions, if only because of his extreme lack of will, which requires some kind of guide. He took up those war games that involve running around wooded areas trying to shoot paint at your opponents. While practising this sport he fell in with a semi-legal paramilitary organisation. To describe its members I want you first to think back to one of those animal programmes on television; you must have seen that frog (which lives in South America, a continent that vies with Australia in the field of extraordinary fauna): the one that expands its chest with air and at the same time makes an unpleasant croaking sound. Having fixed that image in your mind, you will find it easier to picture how these people threw out their chests and went around making unpleasant utterances. Now one of these croaking frogs, who had retired as a major from a distinguished career in protecting rocks, had a slight penchant for young lads such as this barman who had been instructed to wring my neck, and his desires did not go long unrequited. On one occasion, when his wife left to stay with a friend, the major had my would-be executioner come and spend the night with him. Early the next day, they were woken by the sound of the wife who had returned early and the barman had only just enough time to dive under the bed before she entered the room. 'Oh dearest,' she said, 'you'll never guess the embarrassment I've been put to.' The major affected to be interested. 'My dearest friend, who I have known since my schooldays, has just discovered that her husband has homosexual tendencies, that he invites youths to their home while she's away. They have been arguing all the time I was there, and I had to make up an excuse to leave early.' The major, forgetting his friend under the bed, was outraged: 'And he's a judge! What kind of example is that to give the youth of today? Small wonder the country is in the mess it's in, with people like that in charge! Just another example of the moral decay that has set in, since we have started pandering to all society's rejects rather than rewarding hard work and principles.' 'I quite agree! At least I chose a real man all those years ago. She might be married to a judge, but think of the shame if this ever got out.' At this point she drew close to the bed and unfortunately the point of her heel pressed down on the tip of the barman's finger which was barely protruding. There was a sudden scream and the luckless lover was obliged to reveal himself.

Now the wife was enjoying a lustful middle age and she had already sized up the baby-faced youth before her. Nor was she illiberal in her attitudes or lacking in a sense of humour. When she had managed to control her laughter she said: 'I have slept very little at my friend's house so I have decided to spend the rest of the day in bed. If you two don't want anyone to hear about this, I suggest you both join me.' So all three returned to bed and the busiest of the three was the unfortunate barman. When eventually he was allowed to leave he was unsure which had been put to greater use: his cavity or his protrusion.

But fate is often doubly cruel and, in this case, had chosen a deserving victim. The wife was not as discreet as she had promised to be and the behaviour of the major came to the notice of his fellow croaking frogs, who considered it extremely unmanly. After some deliberation, they decided only to reprimand him, given his status and generous donations to party funds, but they thought it prudent to dispatch two of their members to frighten the youth into eternal silence. These two individuals were squarely built from sullen sinewed flesh like close-cropped clones from the factory of hate; they had all the elegance of a bulldog, and an expression that looked as though it could be programmed. Having waited patiently in the bar all evening, they quickly moved to the backdoor in order to ambush the barman. Just as my executioner tightened his clammy hands around my neck, he was pounced upon and shoved up against the wall, where with every blow they instructed him to keep his poncy self out of their way in future and not to breathe a word to anyone. Naturally he couldn't hold on to me for long, and as he let me go, one of the thugs shouted from behind me: 'Get that parrot – he must be worth something!'

I was just in time, and immediately I started my cumbersome flight back to the bell-less bell-tower to attempt once more to change myself. I had discovered how dangerous it is to be so valuable a commodity as a singing parrot.

CHAPTER FOUR

Thought Without Speech

The author exchanges chatter for silence, but feels alone. He is still capable of foolishness. Aloof from other people's relationships, he is not above interfering in them. Real comfort at last is not enough to overcome his yearning for his former human form.

I took the puzzle down,
trainbound, in the car,
supine smoothly bedslung,
amongst the rushed flow
of human integers,
the indivisible cells of thought,
I turned it over,
felt its weight,
and duly pondered in the bath
its full extent, its width, its length,
the inner puzzles, part results
and still ...
it fled, it teased, it entertained
and cursed perhaps my arrogance
and cried: 'give up, the arms of ritual
and routine embrace all those
who do not care; suck in
the sordid juices of despair
the ready made realities for the ruled;
let the all-consuming daemon of consumption

quell the inner fires of your humanity,
inscribe its signature of surfeit on a thrombosed heart.'

READER, YOU MAY have guessed that it was not yet my fate to regain my human frame. I will be as brief as possible and introduce you immediately to my feline form.

For a cat it is easy to find a home and I was adopted by a married couple, both university lecturers. He was called Robert Rimescioni and owed his Italian surname to his father who had arrived as a political refugee in the Thirties. Although distinctly English in character and particularly in his intellectual make-up, Robert was a scholar of his father's language and its literature. Still in his early forties, he had risen to the enviable status of Head of Department, a position achieved with truly Machiavellian art; no moral vision cluttered his course to power. Power was the unashamed means to acquire the pleasure of its exercise, its sense of purpose, the comfort of respect and the sedative of security. He used fashionable ideas like battering rams with which to knock down any obstacles to his career. He flirted with left-wing ideas in the Seventies but always stayed within the safety of the British academic world. He had proclaimed revolutionary ardour to admiring students and a temporarily disarmed faculty. When that began to wane he took up feminism with equal vigour. By now well established in his career, he practised positive discrimination against all men, with the exception of himself who he considered exempted by virtue of his virtue. When government directives started to warn against falling standards, he discarded his liberal attitude to students (or at least restricted it to a few of the fairer members of the fairer sex), and became one of the harshest disciplinarians and defenders of academic excellence. He was a man who could never fail in his career, because he was consistently and punctually one year behind every new idea, which he skilfully took up just at the moment it was gaining currency.

At the time I was his feline guest, he was working on an annotated edition of the complete works of Anton-Francesco Doni, a minor Italian satirist of the sixteenth century. Since then, my curiosity has led me to investigate this writer who turns out to be something of a wild character, leading a hand-to-mouth existence, churning out reams of bizarre prose on almost every subject you could imagine. This Doni was not extremely learned, but he knew how to stack up words, play with ideas, to ridicule, to parody. True to his calling, he made fun of everyone including himself, but his vitriol was particularly directed against the scholar and the pedant. So the successful academic was studying the failed artist. The scholar was studying a man who considered scholarship the ultimate folly. Did he enjoy the humour and did he ever consider that it might have been directed at him? Can the pedant understand the anti-pedant? Perhaps inside his mind, which readily accepted rules and categories, and transmitted them on to his students, there was a certain admiration for the man who railed against all the rules and categories of his time.

My real benefactor was his wife, Janice, who immediately left a saucer of milk when she saw me circling aimlessly in the garden, one sunny afternoon. Her career in classical languages had not, formerly at least, been so successful as her husband's. She too studied satire and had recently written on Apuleius' strange and slightly unsavoury masterpiece that attempts to use the profane to create a moral work within the context of that writer's aristocratic and brutally anti-Christian views. Robert would occasionally hold court at his house, *ex cathedra* hold forth, and unfurl phrases like banners marking the position of the legions of his thought. Janice never appreciated his Napoleonic stature; she had admired the image of the man, but now despised the substance: he no longer possessed any words that could surprise her. All marriages tend to exhaust their stocks of conversation, but for those whose careers involve the use of words and ideas, this shortcoming is all the more serious. Their rooms held a bookish silence, or perhaps stuffiness. Even the kitchen had a pedantic edge. I was comfortable and free to wander the rooms of the house of this silent, childless couple. They worked endlessly in their separate studies, in the silence of their thoughts.

I became a creature of habit. Only habit allows reflection. Where there is chatter and bustle, there is rarely thought. Thought abhors the pressures of time. A thought is often born in a moment when all the requirements of reality are being made. It is an unwanted diversion, when catching the bus or arguing with a colleague at work. You have to catch it and store it somewhere, or it will never blossom. What little time we have to think, we fill instead with sound and images; we consume the packaged thoughts of others. Far away. The media package far away thoughts that chatter through our days. A cat, on the other hand, has a great deal of time to think.

I would often go to the front room and jump onto the sill. The images of the road outside would blur and I would sink into my reverie. When a human thinks, it is usually because he wishes to communicate that thought eventually in conversation or through the written word. It is never a completely private thought. It desires an audience. It wants to be received, to be appreciated. Thus it is seldom entirely honest. It may be born in grand style, it may be a mere whimper of a thought squeezed out of an uninspired moment, but it will always change and search for acceptance. It wishes to enhance its owner, to display his wit, knowledge or intellect. It must not be too revolutionary in order to avoid offence or even seeming a little mad. It must not be too conventional in order to avoid being dull or even seeming a little stupid. It is governed by the society into which it is to be received. When a cat (or at least a cat with a human brain) thinks, it thinks for itself. The thought cannot be communicated, it can only expand into its own universe. It is a lonely thought, but it is completely honest. I would often think with no respect for order or coherence. I would consider the abyss that divides us all and wonder at our horrific similarity, our anonymity. Given this human state, it is strange that there are not more megalomaniacs in the world, who desire to rise up and stamp their own image on an age, to transcend their isolation by holding hundreds of thousands of lives in their hands, like Gods on a dull day. Perhaps megalomania is not so unusual, it is a relative state, it is ambition, a desire to control first a mere group of friends or colleagues, and then an organisation, and so on as far as it can go. Perhaps any attempt to externalise ourselves, our thoughts or our desires is an act of megalomania: that is why holy men went into the desert.

Perhaps the greatest works of art were those that were never realised, but remained in their state of innocence just as they were born. In the mind they have no substance, and by taking form in the world they lose all the grandeur of fantasy. A good artist retains something of that fantasy in his work, but never all of it. Most works of art follow some set of rules laid down by the men that dampen hope, by the men that followed the instincts of their megalomania and succeeded, and by the men who turned their thoughts into the right words, said them at the right time and rose through the ranks to positions of power. We all have to compromise with these men, if we are to make any impression.

The paradox is simply this: the philosopher, as we all know, said that to think is to be, but our thoughts also want to be communicated. To think we have to use a language, which has been invented and moulded by endless generations, and then handed down to us. Thought is part of the whole and of history. To communicate is to compromise with the audience or with how we perceive the audience, and thus we are no longer completely ourselves. Or in a sense, to think is not to be, but to belong to others, their culture and their way of seeing things.

A peasant couple lived deep in the woods, and the dense foliage protected them from the noises of other men, from their diseases and wars. They never lacked words or companionship, as the business of survival engaged their minds and tongues in a common cause. Pigs to feed, wood to chop, walls to build, and earth to dig. They knew each other's smells and sounds, and relaxed in them as in their friendly bed of straw. Then one day a perverse fairy with a penchant for sociological experiments waved her wand and they became king and queen of a vast nation.

The peasant-king said: 'Summon my court!' and in came a group of busy men with busy voices: 'The taxes are insufficient', 'The army needs reinforcements', 'Heretics are corrupting the people', 'The harvest is poor.' The peasant-queen complained: her diamonds were too light, her clothes too coarse, her hair too grey, her chin misshapen. On their first night in their beautiful new castle, she heard him snore for the first time, and he smelt the pungent odour of her gases through the crispness of the linen sheets. He understood the endlessness of her desires, and she the dullness of his preoccupations.

The next morning she had their dining table lengthened so that she couldn't hear him burp. He turned so as to avoid looking at her misshapen chin. Then in rushed the courtiers and addressed the peasant-queen. 'Madam, we have discovered a surgeon who is a genius with a scalpel. He can make you even more radiant than you are now: he can put your arse on your face, and he can tie your cheeks up at the back of your neck.'

From the other side of the hall more courtiers arrived and addressed the peasant-king. 'Sire, we have discovered an engineer who can build an enormous chariot of steel that can fly in the sky like a bird. Think of the glory and the stature of a man who could travel in such a machine.'

In spite of the surgeon's craftsmanship, the peasant-king found the peasant-queen increasingly repulsive, and in spite of the peasant-king's aeronautic experiences, the peasant-queen found him increasingly vulgar. They moved to separate rooms, and then to separate wings, and finally to separate towers. But they could take up their telescopes and spy on each other sitting at opposing windows.

They spent so much money on surgery and planes, not to speak of microwave cookers, motorised chariots, sandwich toasters and nuclear bombs, that their subjects became increasingly impoverished, until one day they rebelled. The courtiers ran to see the peasant-queen: 'Madam, the people are at the gate – they are starving!'

'Then let them watch videos!' she replied coolly.

They then ran to the king with the same news, and he, ever the more practical of the pair, simply said: 'Use the machine-guns and send them home.'

The years passed and the couple became ever more recluse. Sometimes they would sit at their windows and stare at each other, angry that the other did not measure up to the ideal required by their status. Then one day the catastrophe occurred. An eagle swooped down and stole the peasant-king's wig. The queen began to laugh and, it is terrible to recount, the stitching in the plastic surgery at the back of her neck came undone and her cheeks fell down the side of the tower stretching all the way to the ground. Every fold in her cheeks represented a year of their reign.

Her laughter turned to tears and she moaned: 'if only I could become a peasant woman again'. The fairy-sociologist heard her plea, and feeling that she had discovered all she wanted to know, waved her wand in order to return them to their former state. But nothing happened, and the fairy had to admit: 'that eyes that have watched television, fingers that have changed channels, and arses that have stayed immobile in cushioned armchairs for hours on end, are all immune to magic. The experiment, I'm afraid, is irreversible.'

After my unfortunate experience in the Brewer's Arms, I had decided to go on the wagon, at least until I regained my human shape. It is after all in the dietary field that humanity demonstrates its innate superiority to the lower species. We should take greater pride in our prodigious ingestion of the widest possible variety of organic matter, which can be mixed together creating an infinite number of possible permutations and presenting us with a greater artistic challenge than that created by these graphic symbols that you are currently deciphering (the alphabet has a miserly twenty-six ingredients from which to create its meagre infinity, while the basic ingredients a cook can call on are almost infinite even before he begins to mix them). Indeed Man in search of a name that would distance himself from his own humanity and put himself, as it were, under the microscope, could have more aptly named himself *homo culinarius* rather than a mere *homo sapiens*, cooking man rather than wise man. But the invention of alcohol must surely be our crowning achievement and folly, for it is with this medicine that we dull the sharp pain caused by having too many brain cells. By confusing the delicate circuitry of the grey blancmange that is the very centre of our sense of existence, alcohol blurs the jagged edges of our perceptions and frees the sweeter interpretations of our inner fantasies.

It may be that westerners spend more on feeding their cats and dogs than several starving countries can afford to spend on feeding themselves, but I'll let you into a secret: the western shopper has been ripped off once again. Okay, so the packaging may be pretty smart these days, but it is still tinned offal and gelatine, and I can tell you it's not a varied diet. I'd taken the pledge. Booze had got me into trouble with the Bacchic freaks, at Thelma's party and in the pub. My life was pleasant apart from the food. An ascetic feline existence which put very few demands upon me. Contentment before a fall. Just when you're thinking that you could go on living like this for the rest of your life, a momentary lapse sets off a string of events that change your life. Or perhaps you do it on purpose, a subconscious rebellion.

One day, having rejected my supper, which seemed more attractive to the flies, I went in search of something better. Now a *real* cat, by which I mean a cat without a human soul, would have answered his instinct and hunted for some fresh meat, but I'm of a gentle and leisurely disposition, and decided that the kitchen was likely to provide me with a more agreeable food supply. I found a glass bowl containing sherry trifle and immediately started to gorge myself. I ate myself to a standstill and lay down beside the empty bowl to sleep a well-earned sleep and allowed my feline gastric juices to digest the sickly matter of my human appetite. While I slumbered happily, my mistress returned with a basketful of oven-ready food. She was extremely distressed to find that one of her few culinary enterprises had somehow managed to be consumed during her absence. Circumstantial evidence pointed the finger of guilt at me, but she would never have convinced herself of such an improbable culprit if she hadn't noticed the globules of cream that weighed down my long and elegant feline whiskers. I was at the time contentedly purring while I swam the delicious voluptuousness of my intoxicated dream. On making her discovery, Janice's mood changed to one of hilarity, such is the power of laughter over both reasonable and unreasonable outrage. Even the most pompous of individuals can be caught off-guard by the improbable situation that brings unversed and unaccustomed laughter bubbling out from its cavernous prison below the vocal cords. Indeed I must digress to illustrate my argument better.

There was a general whose limited intelligence was just sufficient to learn the obscure Masonic rituals by which to make his career. He had been told that the strategic skills of a general are very similar to those of a chess-player, and so decided in retirement to take up the game. He dedicated all his energies to his new-found hobby, and after some months managed to master the moves of the various pieces. He had more trouble, however, finding someone whom he could beat. Eventually he heard about a monkey that had also been taught the basic moves of chess and so he bought the animal. The general sat down to the first game glowing with anticipation at the idea of finally demonstrating his tactical finesse. The monkey, although of undoubted conceptual ability, hadn't quite mastered the human concept of respect for rank and status, and it was probably due to this inability to perceive the more subtle aspects of social propriety that the wretched beast checkmated the even more wretched general in a few moves. The primate had clearly shown his moral and genetic inferiority, and the general lost no time in teaching him the lesson by beating him around the head with his fists. Once this had been done to the general's satisfaction, he set the chess-pieces up again and they commenced the second game. Unfortunately for the monkey, the general was not an easy man to lose to and so, inevitably, he beat him for a second time. When the general saw the effrontery of the animal, he raised his fists to mete out a second and more cruel lesson, but the opposing primate was a quick learner and, anticipating the danger, he reached for the chamber pot that the incontinent general kept beside the bed and put it on his head. When he saw the monkey before him wearing the pot like a helmet, and steadying it with his fist as though he were trying to salute a superior officer, the general's pomposity melted and he began to laugh, and laughing he had to desist from hitting the monkey whose innocent but rigorous logic had fortuitously saved him from a beating.

But Janice was no pompous general and the absurdity of a trifle-eating cat had even less difficulty in dispelling her anger. Her laughter woke me from my stupor, just as Robert came into the room. 'Look, the cat's eaten the trifle!' she cried, pointing to the empty glass bowl. 'Have you been drinking, Janice?' he retorted, affecting an air of irritation. 'What do you mean drinking? I've just got home. I swear to you that the cat must have eaten the trifle; there was no-one else in the house. Besides, you can see the cream around his face.' The husband wasn't interested in the evidence, and seemed to have decided to take this last example of her eccentricity as an excuse to say something that had clearly been on his mind for some time. 'Look Janice, I think you need help, but I don't think I'm the one that can help you. I have tried to stick by you, but you are incapable of listening to anything I say.' The residual cheerfulness caused by my antics was fast disappearing from Janice's face: 'So what are you getting at?'

'Come on, I've had enough of this farce. Can't you see that there is absolutely no communication between us at all? It is time for us to call it a day and for each to go their separate way.'

'That's okay,' she replied, 'you can leave any time.'

'And leave you in this state? That would be irresponsible. You must go to your mother's or seek professional help. You've got to face up to that fact that you have a problem, you're quietly cracking up, talking to the cat, trying to feed it trifle, drinking in the daytime. I know you're disappointed about the reaction to your articles on Apuleius; that's why you've got to get away to sort yourself out.'

'Very thoughtful of you, but I haven't been drinking. I'll feed the cat trifle now that I know that it likes it, and it never occurred to me to be disappointed about that article – I liked it.'

'Look, I might as well be clear about this: I've promised Sally that I'm going to marry her as soon as I can get a divorce. In fact I'm going to ring her now and ask her to come round so that we can argue the whole thing out in a civilised and adult fashion.' He left the room and, feeling a little sorry for Janice, I dived into her lap to give her some comfort. As she stroked my back, she spoke her thoughts aloud, unaware that I could comprehend them. 'I don't mind splitting up from the bastard, but why should *I* leave? On the other hand, I don't think I can put up with the messiness of this argument – he's bound to put up a big fight for his own interests, while simulating fairness to all with his perennial air of a committee chairman.' It was probably in that moment that I decided to try my hand at being a *deus ex machina*, to meddle in the natural course of history, and to fight on Janice's side, given that she had no fight in her.

Sally, good-looking and energetic, a finalist on one of Robert's courses, appeared in the evening, slightly nervous but clearly steeled for a confrontation. She strode into the room oozing determination and youth, commodities that Robert found attractive and Janice irritating, but for the same reason: their own stocks were getting low. The meeting started punctually; Robert did indeed have an instinct for chairmanship and insisted on Sally not interrupting Janice, as she raised her objections to this or that proposal. Everything was conducted in the most impeccably civilised manner. But fortunately I was feline enough not to be held back by such niceties, and when Sally asked where the bathroom was, I was ready to make my move.

I ran after her, caught her at the top of the stairs and, after pausing a second to recompose myself, I said in conversational tone: 'So you and Robert are to be wed?' The girl spun round looking for her interlocutor. 'Don't be shocked. It's me, the cat that's talking to you.' She drew her breath, unable to utter a word, a cry of surprise or a call for help. 'No, don't be scared, please. I come as a friend, I have come to warn you.' She continued to stare at me, her powers of speech, and perhaps of thought, totally frozen by her amazement. 'You are of course wondering how a cat could possibly speak, but the fact of the matter is that I am in reality a man in a cat's body. I was once one of Janice's lovers, and because I was unfaithful to her, she turned me into a cat. It is a cruel punishment, but not as cruel as her treatment of Robert's lovers. They have been turned into the basest and unluckiest of animals, such as a frog whose pond bordered with a motorway, a starling that nested in the cooling tower at Windscale, a snail that answered to the exotic name of *escargot*, not to mention several worms in a fisherman's bag.' If her feet had been nailed to the floor, she would not have been more securely fastened to that spot. 'I'm sorry if I have been too blunt with you, Sally, but I am telling you this for your own good. The dreadful truth is that Janice is one of the most accomplished witches this side of the Middle Ages'. This announcement was punctuated by the girl gasping for breath, as though she required a large amount of oxygen to digest so enormous a revelation. 'My only advice to you is to run. It may already be too late, but I would run and steer clear of this house.' The advice took a few seconds to have its effect, but when it came it was instantaneous: she darted down the stairs as though she had all the guardians of hell at her heels. When the front door slammed behind her, the whole house shook.

After a few minutes, I re-entered the sitting room, slightly shamed-face because of my perverse meddling. Janice and Robert were sitting in total silence, unable to communicate their surprise at Sally's unexpected behaviour. The following day Robert returned almost suicidal. His lover was still in a state of total shock, unable to speak, but as everyone knew about her relationship with Robert, he was now being held responsible for some unspeakable crime. I regretted my own fervid imagination, which had hardly respected the poor girl's feelings. Robert found that the edifice of his reasonableness, which had been carefully constructed over many years, suddenly came crashing down; the goddess of gossip was running riot and ruining the ambitions for which that edifice had been built. He was alone, surrounded by broken dreams, by fallen fantasies. Now, our fantasies are like our farts: we are not offended by the smell of our own, but only by that of other people's; so let us not be to harsh with Robert. His ambitions were no different from our own: he wished to be loved, respected, wealthy and successful.

But his problems didn't end there. The whole affair had repercussions that I could never have foreseen. Sally had been transformed from model student into a suitable case for counselling. Traumatised, and everyone knew who was responsible. The head of the French Department was a man of a considerable intellect that expressed itself through long forceful silences. Nobody was quite sure what he thought about, but everyone was convinced that his disdainful muteness concealed the ultimate truth on every subject. He had destroyed even the most cogent arguments of his colleagues with his withering silences, and they in turn had learnt to respect and fear him. When he heard about the incident, he deigned to engage in the vulgar practice of verbal communication for just long enough to imply to the head of the German Department that Robert had used violence against his young student in the frustration of his debauched passion. The Head of the German Department was as loquacious as his colleague was taciturn, and he quoted his reliable source to the Spanish and Russian departments, and rumour spread through the neat compartments of modern European vernacular and far beyond. Distant echoes were heard in Organic Chemistry and the Forestry Research Unit, where Robert's name wasn't known and he was referred to as 'some guy in modern languages'. Rumour is the most powerful and insidious of enemies because there is no right of appeal; it is impossible to stop acquaintances and plead that there is no truth in the accusations, and this would, in any case, be construed as the definitive proof of guilt. Nor is Rumour necessarily related to any particular maliciousness; it is its attractiveness as a story that gives it strength. Unfortunately for Robert the accusation against him had much of that kind of sensationalism. Had he not been the great feminist, had he not chided many of his colleagues for rampant machismo, had he not flaunted his deeply felt principles, constantly relating them to every aspect of society, and beating his breast in an act of contrition, confession and expiation of his manly sins? And now he stood accused of rape, a hideous crime that was accompanied by that of stubborn hypocrisy.

If he could not rescue his career, he desperately wanted to rescue at least his friends. He visited them assiduously; he insisted they came round. He chattered, but he could not think and he could not listen. He began to mix his drinks like he mixed his ideas and vice versa in a spiral, as he spun off, freed from the strictures of his image and the ambitions that had required it. People began to avoid him. When he called on them, they kept him at the door – they were too busy, they were sorry, he must come round, but they hadn't time at the moment.

People enjoy scandal. They click their tongues, while they wallow in the blissful relief of discovering that others appear more evil than they secretly fear they might be themselves. The more people are unhappy with their own conduct, the readier they are to believe bad conduct attributed to others. They bask for a short while in the glow of their relative virtue. They never think for themselves in these cases, but always with the whole of society. They accept the standard judgement, as it allows them to relax in the pool of common thoughtlessness. The simple fact was that Robert's nature, though ambitious, was always gentle; the improbability of the accusation was never considered.

Robert, on the other hand, was isolated in the knowledge of his innocence. For the first time in many years, he was forced to address his thoughts to himself, because no-one was interested in them any longer, no matter how he dressed them up. Adversity is a great liberator. And defeat an even greater one. His sense of outrage was subdued; he began to see that he too was guilty, not of rape, but of thoughtlessness. When he had been young, he had loved humanity from his heart. He had cared. When he read about Vietnam or Eritrea, his anger bounded out of his heart and filled the air with anguish and with helplessness. He felt. But then his humanity had moved to his intestines and become bound up with the act of survival. The daily processes of feeding his needs had hijacked his desire for other peoples' betterment. He had continued to argue over Vietnam or Eritrea, but he was more interested in events proving his predictions and the subtlety of his arguments than in his fellow men, the abstract forms he never saw except upon a television screen, being liberated from their plights. He thought alone and thought his way back to the innocence of his youthful ideas. Perhaps he had sought a young lover to recapture youth. Poor fool! He thought that he had had something to say, but there are few who have such fortune, and such fortune has more to do with the timeliness of ideas than with any intrinsic ability.

Janice was sensitive to his plight. They put up a common front and discovered a certain warmth in their silent solidarity. She too began to question her seriousness, her academic integrity. She realised that intellectuals search not the truth, but original thought, which can carry their initials on it, the mark of their powers, the expression of their status. By their originality, intellectuals hope to identify the truth with themselves, to stun and illuminate humanity at the same time. But the truth is rarely original, so by attempting to possess the truth, intellectual individualists exclude themselves from it. Truth, like goodness, is often banal, or perceived as such by those who live on a surfeit of ideas.

After these momentous events in our household, I settled into a pleasant rut. I would sneak around more or less unwatched, observing how people behaved and trying unsuccessfully to understand both the humdrum and the occasionally erratic movement of their lives. The range of events and absurdities that exposed themselves to my silent feline philosophising was as vast as it was disturbing, but I am only going to tell or rather retell a story I overheard. One of my favourite spots was above a cupboard in a Vietnamese restaurant. They were kind to me, gave me scraps and let me have a free run as long as I didn't get too close to the food. One late afternoon as they were tidying up, they started on one of their favourite subjects: the evils of the communists and the North Vietnamese. After a while, the old grandmother, who usually sat silently in the corner, interjected: 'You can say what you like about the communists, but I can tell you a story of at least one who was a very good man'.

'Come on, let's hear it then'.

'It was in the Sixties. He was a young man living in the North and his name was Kien Bao. The Americans had just started to bomb the North heavily, and he felt he had to volunteer to defend the country, as young men are often keen to do. At the time he was very much in love with a girl called Phuon, so he told her of his decision, which she considered the only honourable one to take, and he departed for the war. Again like many young men, he thought that the war would be over quickly and he would achieve many great deeds that would make Phuon love him even more than he assumed she already did. War turned out to be bitter, brutal and, what was worse, interminable. The years passed without him being able to return home. He constantly wrote to Phuon, but never received a reply. This did not worry him too much because it was very difficult to get letters to the front line and many were lost along the way. All his comrades died and so did the ones that came later, yet still he lived on as though protected for some future task. And all the time he remained faithful to Phuon. Even after years among the heavy smells of the jungle, close-living and death, he could remember the warm perfume of her body as they made love on the beach shortly before he left.

'Finally, after many years of sorrow, he returned home to discover that Phuon had married a high-ranking official, who had done his best to keep Kien at the front. She wanted nothing to do with him and he was devastated. He had always assumed that their love had been as important for her as it had been for him. He lived for many more years as a recluse, writing poetry about the cruelty of the enemy, the wastefulness of his generals (wasteful with the lives of young men) and his love for the bright-eyed, fresh-smelling woman who should have shared his days and nights in the ideal life he had not been allowed to live. This seemingly purposeless activity was his therapy, his only way to believe again that there could be beauty in this world – that what he thought and what he did still had some sense. The enemy had been powerful in arms and even more powerful in propaganda – his unpublished writings were a personal record of the trauma of war. When more years had passed, he started to go out and search for Phuon. He found that every few days she visited a certain park with her children and he started to go there too. And after several months, she allowed him to talk to her. "Kien," she would say, "why haven't you got a woman, why haven't you married? What we had was just a kid's thing. We were young, far too young to fall in love – to settle down. That was just fun."

'He couldn't bear to hear her say that. She had kept him alive. Only the hope of seeing her again had made him careful, when the cruelty of war would otherwise have made death seem preferable. He had lived for her. No, she replied, he had lived for his ideal image of her. Any young girl that he had left behind would have done. He was, she claimed, in love with the idea of being in love. She had no time for poetry either. She did not want to hear of his love for her, and still less did she want to hear of his war. He hated what she said, but bathed in the sweetness of her company. He loved every little thing about that woman with a passion that excluded everything else – even his memories of the war for as long as she was with him. She told him that her husband was not a particularly good man, but he wasn't a bad one either. He was very ambitious, and could provide well for her and her children.

'Kien's months of frustrated happiness did not last. Suddenly Phuon no longer came to the park. First he thought she had decided to avoid him, because he knew they were close to becoming lovers again. She had decided not to see him because she was weakening, he was sure of it. But then came worse news: she had cancer and was very ill. And then worse news still: her husband's clique had fallen from grace and he was under arrest for anti-state activities. He had to help, but he didn't know how. He went to where the compounds of higher officials stretched out of the city. He walked for miles in the heat, sometimes aimlessly, hopelessly, sometimes with a method, taking a block at a time. He knew that her house would have guards outside, but he hadn't decided how he could get in. Occasionally he was stopped and questioned, and finally he was picked up. He was thrown in the back of a smart jeep. In poor countries as in rich, the secret services and police forces always have the best. He sat opposite two officers who studied him dispassionately. "What are you doing here? What are you looking for?" "A sick woman," he said. "I know you," said one of the officers. "You're Kien, a veteran of the war. We thought you weren't interested in women. You never looked at a prostitute or even a country girl whose father needed protection. You wept at the terrible things you saw, but you did not hold yourself back. You fought with the rest of us. You were one of us, and yet you were not like us. At first, I thought you too gentle to be a fighter, but later I realised that it is not caring about yourself that makes a good fighter – and you really didn't care about yourself." The veterans hugged each other, and Kien explained his situation. "To get into Phuon's house you'll need a uniform," said the officer, "of the highest possible rank. General Tong is about your build and is on leave. We'll pick up his uniform from the barracks." Like laughing schoolboys organising a prank, they shot off in the jeep for the barracks. The officers were hooting uncontrollably when Kien had the general's uniform on. "Quiet," he said, "or I'll cancel all leave," and the officers practically fell in a heap of uncontrollable hilarity. When they reached Phuon's house and the guards approached, Kien's hands started to shake: he had fought in the jungle for fifteen years, he had been frightened, but he had never shown any physical signs of fear. Authority was another thing. He hated authority and it frightened him. The officers, on the other hand, were perfectly relaxed; they appeared to have calculated the risks and decided that they were negligible. If anything, they were having difficulty in suppressing a snigger at the continuing absurdity of Kien in a general's uniform. The guards waved them through.

'In the house, Kien entered Phuon's bedroom alone and found her lying in bed. She was pale and clearly dying. Kien felt his own vigour draining out of him, as though he was becoming a different kind of being or animal – one that could no longer feel. The sensitive man was feeling insensitive. He sat on the bed and stared at Phuon. She, too, smiled a little at the incongruity of the situation, and held out her hand. "Kien," she said, "very few are as lucky as I have been in life. Very few have been loved, and even fewer have been loved as I have been loved by you. I don't think I ever deserved such love, and in coming to love you, I felt even less deserving of you. That is why I stopped coming to the park." Tears ran down Kien's face, but he wasn't really feeling anything. The one element of hope, however vain or even morbid that hope had sometimes seemed, was now fading out of his life on the bed before him. When he spoke, his voice was dry and harsh: "I cannot live if I don't know that you are living somewhere." "Don't speak like that, Kien – I have a job for you. My husband, if he survives, will be in prison for a long time, so my three children will be without a father. I want you to go to the state orphanage and collect them. I want you to be the father." Kien fell on his knees and kissed her hand: "Thank you, Phuon. Now I have a purpose. I will be a good father, and when I look into their eyes, I will see your eyes – I will see you continuing to live in them." He lay in her weak embrace for a long time, until the officers knocked on the door and asked him politely to take his leave. As they returned to the jeep, one officer clapped him on his back, "You're a dark horse, Kien. I thought you weren't interested in women." They laughed, and Kien smiled stupidly, thankful to but distant from his friends.

'Kien was true to his word. He brought up Phuon's children as well and as lovingly as any other father. Now he was more relaxed, and he started to publish stories about the War, which became famous and earned him respect and wealth. But he always mourned Phuon and the life he had not been able to live.'

The old woman's relations laughed and shrugged, unconvinced by the story of the good communist, very much I suspect as people laughed and shrugged when they heard the story of the Good Samaritan. In the real world, human beings are not like that – they need a motive, a healthily selfish motive, before they can do anything. Any utilitarian philosopher or Thatcherite can tell you that. And by following your selfish will, quite miraculously you end up doing the best for the greater good. What a wonderful world free of difficult moral decisions! But I in my cat-like state questioned this. It seemed to me that utilitarians are the living disproof of their own simple faith. If they were just to get on with their own selfish needs, they wouldn't go around proselytising everyone with their absurd ideas. Indeed, my reaction to the love story of Kien and Phuon was far from cynical. I have to confess that I was very moved and – you're going to think me a real sop – it was something of a revelation. Suddenly I realised that there is such a thing as *nobility of the soul* – that goes beyond and is obscured by the rush of self-fulfilled consumerdom and the crazed seeking of elusive pleasure (it would make more sense, if it weren't so elusive). In the simple story of this soldier's passion not for glory, promotion or wealth, but for the love of a single other irreplaceable human being, I saw that life comes to those who look for other things. He had fought gloriously enough to win the respect of his comrades, his writings had made him money and, albeit only briefly and illegally, he had been promoted general and heard the heels of other soldiers snap before his authority. Love had guided him there by making him disregard all other things.

Things at home seemed to confirm my new thoughts. Robert and Janice were now getting on better than they probably ever had. And now all the routes to betterment seemed barred for ever, now the divine self-interest of the utilitarians had little purpose in their lives, they seemed a great deal happier. They began to communicate and they began to laugh. They could laugh at the head of French, perceiving as they did that his silence hid not profundity and intellectual rigour, but merely a terrible crushing emptiness. They laughed at the head of German, whose garrulousness only intended to please, but always ended up irritating others. Above all they laughed at themselves, at the importance they had attached to articles no-one reads, to principles everyone wears on their sleeve but rarely cares a deanship for, and to the esteem of others who have no esteem to give, so desperately are they trying to win it for themselves. They realised that, in a world of absurdities, not to speak of the civil wars, famines and natural disasters, they had had the great good luck to end up with well-paid jobs, long holidays, freedom to follow their intellectual interests, students who were generally pleasant and wanted little more than decent marks, and a cellar stocked with some very reasonable red wines. And they had themselves.

The talk of communism may have been responsible for a dream that deeply disturbed me. Janice had left me her customary bowl of sherry trifle – just as I like it with lots of colouring and a deliciously synthetic feel to it. I had stretched out in front of the fire with the wonderful feeling that the world for all its great disappointments is a really pleasant place if you can just get the knack of contentment. A deep sleep followed and conjured up in my imagination a great cathedral, a magnificent stone edifice in the Gothic or possibly neo-Gothic style dedicated not to Christianity but Socialism. Its mystery differed from mine; it was mass, majestic, universal, stone-hard, static, I was small but living. Red heroes buried in the marble floors recalled the cost of so great an edifice, the silent echo of the vaults made hollow hope, but hope remained in the warm-lit images of martyred dead the glass projected upon the grey-stone wall.

The coloured segments of the rose described the greatest story of all, of how a land was ruled by a despotic monster and how he was destroyed. The beast breathed fire from cavernous nostrils, napalm rained down with assorted weaponry, explosives, defoliants, dioxins, Agent Orange, neatly packaged with serial and identification numbers painted on in clear white lettering, ciphers of death that splintered in the rage released from their contents. Every day the citizens had to sacrifice their young men and so much of their hard-earned produce that they were left in poverty. Sometimes the monster would demand a little less and they could extend their city. Then the monster would destroy all with a couple of blows of his tail made of articulated steel rings of decreasing size. He also used his tail to beat out the rhythm of work, as he insisted that all should work incessantly, even if their occupations were purposeless. He would increase and decrease the rhythm according to his whim. But worst of all, he demanded to be worshipped as the Only-Possible-Way-Of-Doing-Things. Long ago he had spoken to chosen philosophers and had laid down Ten Commandments:

1. Thou shalt obey.
2. Thou shalt not kill, except when instructed by the monster, in which case shalt thou kill men, women and children as quickly and efficiently as thou canst.
3. Thou shalt covet everything and grab as much as thou canst, as long as thou shalt render unto the monster that which is the monster's.
4. Thou shalt not concern thyself with the poor as thou hast them with thee always.
5. Thou shalt consider all those who deny that the poor shall always be with us as sworn enemies of the monster, and accept that they must be destroyed along with their blasphemies.
6. Thou must love the monster and never take his name in vain.
7. Love not thy neighbour as he competes with thee for what the monster has so graciously left.
8. Believe in the monster for the monster is the truth, and the truth is the accepted truth that he writes daily in return for the young men and riches that are

sacrificed to him. This is not the truth of the past, nor is it the truth the future; it is the unquestionable and monster-given truth of the present.

9. Serve the monster well and he shall probably not crush thee.
10. Dream not of better things, as that which is must be.

Then came a bearded prophet armed only with knowledge, with the knowledge of things as they could be. He said the Only-Possible-Way-Of-Doing-Things was sick in spite of his fiery nostrils, that he was consumed by an inner contradiction: that complex, cabalistic sums were tearing at the machinery of his limbs, and he foretold the coming of a knight who would smite the monster with a flaming sword. The prophet died before the saviour came on his white charger, lanced the tyrant through his mechanical heart and severed his head with the blade of fire. Unfortunately the people, broken by years of slavery, built another monster and called him the People's Leviathan and worshipped him in the name of the liberating knight and the great prophet that had heralded his coming. Others say the monster was never slain, but was the Hydra. For every head the knight hacked off, another grew, breathing more fire and taunting the noble foe. Soon the flat and desert land was strewn with dismembered heads, each fierce expression pointing in a different direction, so that it was impossible to move across the contested plain without being directly stared at by a hundred pairs of steely lifeless eyes. The saviour had to withdraw, his limbs sapped of all their strength. He then retired to a lonely cave with a few remaining followers, there to plot the impossible again. He always felt close to the day when he would return victorious to the plain, but never fixed the date on which to storm the land in which the titan ruled. Still others claimed that it was a knight who was slain but always returned again and again. If burnt in the monster's breath or mauled by the monster's synthetic claws, he would reappear in another shape. The endless battle would seem to be won, now by one combatant, now by the other, but each would snatch victory from defeat and return with greater will. Thus the Manichaean myth was born.

I woke from my dream in a terrible sweat. Which was the dream? My comfortable cat existence or the real world of struggle, where I would only be an insignificant individual in the crowd, but nevertheless part of something important. Perhaps *nobility of soul* was to be found there – fighting with many others against the monstrous oppressions of this world. I had to divest myself of my cat-like complacency, and get back into the real world. The choice cannot only be between living through the senses or surrendering to complete reclusiveness. Surely life could be a mixture and a balance. Adventures awaited, but as I hastened off, I little thought again how any change could easily be for the worse. The value of a comfortable and complacent life should not be underestimated nor lightly discarded.

CHAPTER FIVE

Nel Mezzo del Cammin

The author encounters his most frightening transformation. An encounter with death, and he searches for words to match the tragic tale. Fotis, far from being the evil temptress of ancient tales, reveals her beneficent nature and her love of humanity.

Deathly, the sucking sea
assails the slope of shifting sand
and drags me on.
Silent wanderer
it hugs the lands,
that great quantity of unknown sleep.

It waits watchingly and is watched.
How good it is to see
and not to touch
with screaming soul
the long, gull-grey, gull-bobbing swell.

– BUILD HIGH THE CASTLES of your desire – says the flagging master of my fantasy as I face up to the most daunting adversary. I can picture you, you last-laughing, shambling caricature. We fear you, but what we scribblers fear most is your triteness – and ours. For we always come round to you in the end. Have our pens not run dry? We build our castles high and you'll not conquer them; starkly cut against the sun, they shall be shiny-rimmed shadows, gems of our forever madness. Nor is it any poetic genius that keeps the high and hard-walled fortress fantasy impregnable to your relentless flood, but simply the repeatability of ideas. Destroy a thought and someone will rethink it. So why make such a show with your grinning skull and rattling gait; you cannot break this well-buttressed structure of our insubstantiality, although new owners constantly refashion it and paint new follies on its inner walls.

Reader, I have reached the middle of my story, the darkest days of my strange journey and my final metamorphosis. Lost in the woods, will my words measure up to these anguished scenes or will some rhetorical flourish undermine the tragic content of my dance with death? Let me introduce the next animal form I was obliged to wear, by saying that the flight of the vulture is similar to that of an eagle only when seen from a distance. My wide and powerful wings carried me smoothly on the current of air that swelled from the dark world below, but in my twisted entrails I felt the ever tauter knot of evil. Of all my metamorphoses, this was the one that most affected my essence, my human soul. I was driven by a terrible instinct to gorge myself on carrion: dead meat the object of my strong night-hovering flight. I had hoped to change back into a human being by taking up the cause. I had gone in search of *nobility of soul*, not to wear it like a badge of honour, but for myself – to prove my own humanity and regain it. Instead, I came upon the most terrible depression. The trouble with class war, however justified, is that, like any other war, it is based on hate of another.

It has been said that each is born with a fixed predisposition to good and bad. Education and the effectiveness of society's laws may alter external behaviour through reason but the inner instincts will remain unchanged. Undoubtedly this idea will have its share of truth, but the story I am about to tell, if it is true, would tend to weaken it. A man of easy temperament, good-natured but apolitical, living in an insular, good-natured but apolitical town, set up a small upholstery business. He was skilled at what he did and soon built up a large clientele. He married, had children and remained true to his good instincts. And still his business grew through good fortune and hard work. The town was expanding and creating greater demand for his services, so he was eventually able to set up a small furniture factory that quickly became a large furniture factory, and a chain of retail stores colonised the country with its brightly coloured logo. Of course much of what he nominally owned was in reality owned by the bank. He had responsibilities and wore with pride the power which derived from them. His body glowed with the sureness of success and his countenance conveyed the clear expressions, the social messages of the man who has achieved and perceives achievement to have come from his own formidable will. What he did not perceive was how he stood alone, challenged by his competitors and his interests divided from those who worked for him. Gone were the heroic days of his enterprise, when he knew all his employees, and he would take his turn to make the tea that they would drink from an oddly assorted collection of chipped mugs. There were unions and strikes; there were price wars and take-over bids. Each day presented smiling and hostile faces, and he was unsure as to which he distrusted most.

His wife said that there had been several burglaries in the area and they should protect themselves. He bought a couple of Alsatian dogs, installed an alarm system and raised the perimeter wall, on top of which he had broken glass cemented in. A group of men who earned their wealth by preying on that of others, who hunted like wolves in a pack, drove past and noticed the high wall topped with broken glass, and were attracted by the unseen house and its unseen treasure. The robbers, too, no doubt carried their own genetic and environmental histories, like the arcane hieroglyphics of an ancient tomb. Our natures are as solid and grey as the grave, hiding the rotting matter of our pasts. But even though we should treat the living as we do the dead, we never do: we reconstruct them in our own image of humanity, and they are the walking shadows of ourselves. An honest man is naive because he believes that most human beings are honest like himself. A dishonest man is devious because he assumes that all people are liars like himself. So anything I say about these people would tell you little about them and only something about myself. I really do not know what moved them to their act of force – evil, adventure, rebellion, fantasy, a love of firearms, unhappy childhoods, dull childhoods, pampered childhoods, a lack of discipline, too much discipline, too much TV, greed, a hate of work, sadism, undirected anger, anti-social DNA, food poisoning, bad diet, something in the water, failure to attend Sunday school or lack of moral teaching or too much religious teaching which caused natural emotions to be repressed – the choice is yours, if you are rash enough to make one. They had little difficulty in breaching the defences of the house-fortress and kidnapping his wife. They broke in one evening as the family was collecting around the television; gun-toting they acted out the scene with precision and a narcissistic awareness of their own dramatic image. As they went dragging the wife, they shouted orders and informed the helpless husband that they would soon be in touch. He, however, had been struck by a single detail – the fact that one of the raiders was black. At a stroke, he divided himself from another large section of humanity, the insidious fear of the perceived insidiousness of the immigrant poisoned his blood, and he would have built his broken-glass-topped wall around the entire coast. He was incapable of seeing the irrelevance of this detail to his personal tragedy or logically appraising the fact that the other four kidnappers were white or what the Americans call Caucasian (only a country with very little history could be so sure of pre-history, and presumably imply that all Europeans have descended from hillbillies who one day decided to leave their lands between the Black and Caspian Seas to go and populate a continent – don't they know that Europe was always the destination of peoples who had run out of room? – it was the original New World and is still capable of absorbing more).

Once the ransom had been paid, the wife was dumped, bound and badly beaten, on a lonely country road. Presently a vicar came along and heard the woman's muffled cries and looked at her with his habitual expression of pursed-lipped priggishness. But as he was afraid that the bandits could still have been around and felt that she was probably in some way responsible for her predicament, he decided to continue on his way on the other side of the road. Not long after, a mullah came and he too heard her laments. He wanted to help, but he too thought that she must have been responsible for her situation. 'These white women lead such dissipated lives that nothing would surprise me. Besides I mustn't be late for this morning's book-burning session,' and he too continued along the other side of the road. The next person to come along was not a priest of any kind, but a man of two races and two religions. His mother was Welsh and his father an Arab seaman, who had lived in Cardiff, close to the dockside, an imperial inlet, a human staging post. Indeed the only redeeming feature of empires is that they force cultures to meet, to measure up to each other, they are the locomotives of history that drive the peoples of this world towards their common humanity, negative instruments of a positive ideal. This man's father had been British enough to be conscripted in the First World War and eventually to occupy a corner of a foreign field, but inflicted enough foreign-ness on his widow for her house to be burnt down in the race riots of the Twenties. Since then the son, this modern day Samaritan or wandering Jew, had moved from town to town, a homeless outsider who had never learnt the arts of self-pity and bitterness. He had nothing to pin him down to one part of humanity or to cut him off from another; he possessed no property, but kept his human instincts whole. He blasphemed in more than one religion, but there was more gentleness in his bad manners than in the smooth vowels of well-practised practitioners of politeness. He lived off the charity of whores and thieves, he warmed his blood with strong alcohol and beat his brain with powerful music. His doubts came not from apathy, but from a rejection of sin: 'there are only desires that wish to be fulfilled'. He built his own amoral moral code based on his own absence of hate. It would not have worked for all, but it worked sublimely for him. He took the good from both religions and criticised neither.

Any surplus wealth he spent on his one passion: tattoos, which by then covered his entire body. On his chest a large two-headed bird of prey swooped, its claws extended as if to catch up its prey or carrion. One head was that of an eagle, the other that of a vulture. Stretching the full length of his back, four snakes intertwined and at both ends they had a head that flickered a forked tongue. Like the four great religions, they pulled upwards and downwards, tightening the knot of fear.

Without reflection he untied the suffering woman and made her as comfortable as possible, and then ran down the road to call for help.

But as luck would have it, this outsider had, like many who live on the margins of society, a police record. He had partaken of illegal substances, smashed his substance on the sharp needles of chemical substance – in a word, a junky. Given his natural diffidence towards the champions of our property, he left before their arrival, but they soon matched his fingerprints with those found in the area. The police inspector informed our businessman about the arrest of the man, an 'immigrant', in connection with his wife's kidnapping.

The man without a race, the outcast from the desert, was the only evidence they had. The police were convinced of his guilt for two simple reasons: he did not belong anywhere, and no alternative theories presented themselves. Their injustice was driven by a desire for justice, which was both professional and of a genuine nature. They needed to believe in themselves as arbiters of justice, and more generally they needed to believe that justice was possible.

There were other reasons why the police inspector was particular keen to obtain a conviction. The crime, after all, had been committed against a citizen of substance. So while the suspect protested his innocence and claimed to have been the one who called the police and ambulance to the scene, the inspector was more inclined to believe the hard evidence provided by the forensic department. The businessman begged the inspector to have the outsider beaten to within an inch of his life, and the police, who are nothing if not thorough in these kinds of duties, went an inch too far, and the outsider died at their hands. To hide this death in their custody, the police threw the corpse down an embankment and when it came to rest the body lay along the meridian, the arms splayed to the other cardinal points, as though in an attempt to embrace all humanity. His shirt was torn, revealing the head of the vulture, whose hidden talons tore at his entrails. The moon shone softly on the midnight crucifixion.

How much were the businessman's evil reactions a part of inner instinct for self-isolation and how much the cause of the way we build success in this society? You must agree the man had changed within his essence, he was subject to desires that hitherto he had not experienced. So perhaps the pessimistic philosophers should think again and release man's will from its genetic grip. But what is true is that we often act either for good or bad in an instinctive way. In the first case there usually follows a warm sense of virtuousness at having acted without ulterior motives calculated by our reason, and we call this phenomenon our humanity. In the second case, we disown the evil act and consider it a primordial reflex, a relic from our animal past designed to facilitate our survival. We shift our definition of humanity in order to shift the credit or blame for our actions, while in reality our humanity is neither our reason nor our instinct, but the union of the two. Our instincts are perhaps our individuality, including our instinct to reason, but our instincts are also varied and often in conflict with each other. In my vulture form I made the unpleasant discovery of the evil that was in me. It is in our nature to justify our deeds and choices after they have occurred, to search for motives for our motiveless actions, to model fine thoughts to dignify our gut reactions, but even though our powers of self-illusion seem to have no limits there are moments when our baseness presents itself to us as an unavoidable and unpleasant truth, our bad instincts are laid bare – ah, the shield of our pomposity is split across and the sword of our arrogance is blunted (it is an almost sensuous pleasure to deride pomposity with this pompous and now splendidly discredited metaphor).

But the horrors of my vulture-self were not weepy moments of self-pity driven by a sense of persecution; these were the moments of desperate self-hate, such as when the phantoms of our past scream at us and tear at our diseased souls. Suicide can also be caused by self-pity, but then it is a message to society, to family and friends. It must be realistic enough to be convincing as a message, but should stop short of death which would rob the message's sender of the chance to perceive how the message is received. Suicide induced by self-hate is driven by its own destructive force. It has no message for the world but merely wishes to annihilate its own existence, to remove its memory. Often those who suffer from the most bitter self-hate are those who expected too much from life, who loved it too much. They too can teeter on the brink of suicide for many years as they vacillate between past hopes of what they would be and present disgust of what they have become.

Who knows how and when death comes or who commands this vortex of the unknown? To end oneself is to take control, to shut down the machine rather than let it hurtle on dangerously until it crashes against some unknown obstacle. Suicide is both courage and cowardice. The more courageous the spirit, the more fearful the body. Despair carves out a lucid plan, the body freezes in instinctive fear. I could have flown to a power cable landing just inside the insulators, stretched my long wings to the metal of the pylon and the current would have earthed, dragging my soul with it and reducing my body to roast vulture in a matter of microseconds. I could have flown in front of a vehicle on any of the streets below me. But while I may not have feared death, I feared dying; I feared the impact of death, not the pain but the suddenness.

Deathlonging is powerlessness like unrequited love or the insomniac's desire for sleep. Death, the non-lover or sleep become objects because they cannot be possessed, and they cannot be possessed because they have become objects. The deathlonger leaps into oblivion because he wishes to possess too much, because he wants to be all subject and never object. To live one must also allow oneself to be possessed.

In the Middle Ages, they considered death a leveller, because he comes to all men and women, the untiring harvester who cuts away with brutal and rhythmic inevitability, but to me he doesn't appear so democratic. He is more thorough in his work in some parts of the world compared with others, he is less harsh with the rich, more brutal with the dispossessed. If we are no longer faced with eternity and judgement, if this short life is all, then the difference of a decade or two acquires more importance, the sacrifice of suicide becomes the greater, an act of insane profligacy. Lost, without the means to measure my distance from fixed points, to calculate the co-ordinates of my position, without a compass to know whether the direction of my life was good or bad, I both hated life and feared death, vacillated, suspended in a void of anguish.

Eventually I smelt the smell of death and swooped towards the rooftops. I landed, wrapped myself in the dark cloak of my wings and stared across the street to the mesmeric glare of a shop-window neon light, which displayed in laborious but regular joined-up writing the sober words: *Funeral Parlour*. Such misplaced intimacy in that inappropriate 'Parlour'. Can cadavers speak? What is the parlance of an empty corpse? However we approach death, there is always incongruity, humour and horror. Its absurd finality leads us to absurdly reject its reality, to live as though living was all we had to do and, when death comes coffin-close, to shower it with euphemisms like gaudy wreaths of plastic flowers.

I flew in through the open skylight and descended into a room barely-lit by candles that flickered on the very verge of extinction, light that threatened darkness. Two coffins lay open, one containing a youth and the other the corpulent corpse of a middle-aged man. I hopped a devilish dance towards the elder cadaver, all qualms dismissed and intent upon my supper. With my hooked beak I tore away his shirt and just as I aimed my sharp beak at his bared stomach, the corpse spoke: 'Hold still, malign spirit of the night. I know you, sorceress – you have come in the night to gnaw on my lifeless limbs. Have pity on this dead flesh and leave its disfigurement to the worms and the natural processes of decay.'

'How can you speak?' I said, shaking in my vulture claws and recognising the dead man to be Bacchus. 'But I assure you I am no sorceress, but a transformed man, the victim of my own curiosity and a foolish attempt to play with magic.'

'The ability to speak has just returned, solicited by fear of your vile attempt to chew my guts. I, too, am the victim of my own desires. I fell in love with a young girl, a sumptuous lass of mouth-watering beauty, such hips, such breasts, such comely forms to send even an experienced lover like myself into the paroxysms of adolescent folly. Am I not the high priest of the cult of Bacchus, who is desired by all, the convivial friend of all our pleasures? But the little slut ignored me, rejected all my profferings of profoundest love and laughed in my face. For the absence of one pleasure, all other pleasures dried to dust, crumbled before her steely stare like the brittle sod before the ploughshare's cutting edge. [Bacchus, I have to say, was as grand as ever: the mirthless joviality of his obsession]. The search for pleasure turned to despair and there could only be one cure: possession of the little flirt. She had a boyfriend, a silly youth full of fine ideas about this and that. He played the part of the intellectual, recited poetry, affected innocent love and feigned concern for the unfortunate. She naturally, being young, fell for all that false and sanctimonious sham. How could I compete with such underhand methods? I went to a sorceress and asked for a poison. Then at the next opportune moment I offered to buy the young man a drink and poisoned his glass. What was I to do? He was an obstacle to my pleasure and without that pleasure I would have died of anguish. It was, as they say, him or me, and I had no intention of suffering any longer. But then the sorceress, that perverse spirit, appeared from I know not where and said: "Young man, Bacchus has poisoned your drink!" All eyes turned towards me as I indignantly tried to deny the accusation. "Then drink from his glass," she said, and I, in my confusion and fool that I am, took his drink and gulped down what remained of his Bacardi and coke which has, I might add, a most unpleasant and sickly taste, not by any means a drinker's drink. What moved me to that foolish gesture? Did I think I could disprove the sorceress? What a fickle creature is woman. Had I not paid her for her services, why did she have to ruin my plans? For a whim or to rid herself of an accomplice who knew her evil deeds? But proof of her veracity followed almost immediately when my rival fell stone dead at our feet. I no longer cared about the accusing looks, but with tears in my eyes I begged that heartless woman to give me an antidote, while the prefigurement of my own death lay rigid on the floor and the girl's agony and grief for her lover's untimely demise rang in my ears. I must say that before dying, her screams awoke a distant and long-forgotten feeling of regret. Perhaps I was a little foolish over that foolish girl. Now her lover is my companion in the next coffin and, although I still despise him, if we were to wake from the dead, I would do him no harm.'

'Who was the sorceress?' I asked.

'Fotis,' he replied. At that moment there was a noise up in the skylight and a dove appeared. Its whiteness caught and magnified the feeble light of the candles as it lowered itself by delicate and precise movements of its wings.

'Bacchus, put aside your self-pity, you're not dead but waking from a deep sleep,' said the dove. 'I knew that if I refused your request, you would only go elsewhere to procure the necessary for your diabolic plan, so I gave you a powerful soporific called mandrake in place of poison.'

'Fotis, it's you!' Bacchus cried as he sat up in the coffin, clutching at his face to check that it wasn't some deathly dream. The youth in the other coffin began to stir and Fotis flew over to tell him that his lover already knew he was alive and awaited him outside. 'Lucian, come with me,' she cried, 'I will release you from your ugly transformation.'

She flew up to the skylight and out into the night air. I followed and as I did, I thought how a vulture following a dove resembled a bald old man chasing a lithe young woman, I thought of Bacchus and the girl, I thought of the folly of hedonism untempered by intelligence or spirit. Presently we came to the bell-less bell-tower and landed in the middle of the room where a jar of ointment was already prepared.

'Don't be frightened, Lucian,' said Fotis in a voice soft and warm that seemed to touch the very centre of my being, and relax the tension, the terrible thoughts and fears intertwined in a formless knot, and I only became aware of the terrible force of that tension as it began to weaken, just as one becomes aware of the noise of machinery when it is cut off. 'I am not angry with you – only you have suffered from your tampering with what you could not possibly understand – you are the victim of your own quest for knowledge that you believe to be outside you'.

'Fotis, please help me to remove this black-feathered cloak of death, help me return to my former self.'

'Lucian, how serious this suffering has made you. If you do not like your vulture self, then you must destroy it within yourself.'

'How?'

'Touch the ointment and while you do so, think of humanity – not only of your humanity, but of human love, of generosity.'

'But that is ideal humanity; real humanity is also hate, greed, intolerance and violence.'

'True, but if you wish to take on your original form, it is to the ideal humanity within you and within everybody else that you must look'.

I collected my thoughts as if before God (as though we really did possess some greatness in our soul that satire could not touch, some magnificent utopia ready to rise up through the desolation but for one tiny mechanism, a hidden part that obstructs the whole, as I say, as if before God, whoever he may be); I ignored the brutishness that surrounds us all, considering it a shadow of our wretched fears, the desire for power that derives from weakness and solitude, the perverse desire to achieve unity by attaching the universe to our feet. I then sought out the humility that derives from strength, the desire to fall like a droplet into the lake of humanity, the pleasure of the moment, the beauty of the finite, no more condemned to die every minute of life, because death is no longer feared or desired.

'Love your enemies,' Fotis prompted as she passed the jar of ointment, 'they too have their equal share of humanity'. As I touched the jar I began to change, but less painfully this time. My black feathers began to drop as my body and legs swelled. My ugly, bald and beaked head grew and transformed, my hair grew at prodigious speed, restoring its punkish spikes and pinkish tinge, but I was as naked as the day I was born, restored to my innocence of birth, while retaining all the faculties of an adult. I had to build my ideas anew, perhaps only to arrive at a new kind of cynicism. I had found respect for my troubled species whose form I had just regained and for the planet on which its existence depends, and I could now dedicate my existence to grinding those feelings back into dust. Time, like the desert wind, destroys the finer edifices of our belief in good. The important thing is to have believed. Only a fanatic can always believe, and only a fool can never believe. And both are more dangerous than all the fiends of hell.

Fotis passed me a gown and smiled: 'Have you changed?' she asked.

'A great deal and yet hardly at all.'

'Explain! Unexplained paradoxes sound pretentious.'

'Then this one is simple: my intellectual and spiritual attitude has completely changed. I have wiped the slate clean but over the next months and years I will act much as I did before, driven by my old instincts and making the same mistakes, achieving the same bright moments of humour and pleasure, suffering similar periods of despair.'

'I doubt it. While it is true that experience rarely informs behaviour, yours is not so much an experience as a dream, a revelation if you like, a chance to start again. You were old before your time – a cynic is a cripple if he hasn't once believed in something. Cynicism must be a point of arrival not a point of departure. Go and search out ideas – live your life in its correct order.'

'Fotis, was I the product of my environment, or was I simply a case of bad genetic programming?'

'Dear Lucian, I fear these metamorphoses have exalted your brain. How would I know that; leave that kind of speculation to the experts. I am only a simple sorceress, not a PhD in psychology. I believe that we can only really know ourselves, and that is difficult enough. The way in which we interpret others is as much a reflection of ourselves, of our generosity or our distrust, as it is of their unfathomable reality.'

I never saw Fotis again after the evening in which I returned to my human form. I often think of her protective spirit. She was my lover and my teacher, stern and forgiving, sensual and divine, generous but incapable of closeness, paradoxical but no pretentious sophist.

CHAPTER SIX

My Story Chases its Tale

The author takes a pause in order to digress, stretch his restored limbs and prepare for some heavy debate. Or some would say that he loses the plot.

Dir udirò di lontani scogli,
travagli sentirò di intime voglie;
racconta di continuo quel letterato
convinto, gira e rigira e l'amore e'l fato.
Proclama e declama l'utopico stato,
prova e disprova l'ultimo significato
di questa e quell'altra vita.

Lo sento, lo seguo,
lo s'impara, lo si cita.
Ho messo le mani nell'intreccio del suono,
ho intriso le dita nell'intrico dell'uomo
e delle donnesche esistenze.
Ho perso il punto dove tutto s'annoda.
Credenze, sentenze, esperienze,
succube sarò di quelle alla moda.

THIS IS THE MOMENT for my story to take a pause and pick up a few threads of my sorry woes.

On my return to my human self, I went in search of wisdom, or rather of those wiser than I. Who knows which has been the real me, or indeed the better me? The man who set off on an intellectual journey might have been slightly wiser than the man who was metamorphosed into diverse animals, but he might also have been considerably duller. Is it wisdom that turns the erratic and imprudent youth into the moderate middle-ager, or is it fear, property and compromised beliefs? Maybe I was a better man when I was making an ass of myself – when sex and drink and instant unthinking gratification were the only things I went in search of? So what's so wrong with that? I paid a price – I made a fool of myself, like so many others. I leave judgement to the reader. Did the ladder go upwards or down into a sanctimonious pit? Which is more important, the before or the after? Too many questions? Then consider this nightmare I recently had.

With a heavy tick the thin red second-hand chased the slower and heavier black hands around the plastic clock. The doctor's waiting room. In silence the punters held their diseases like drawn breath. They waited and wanted to return to former wholeness, to lost sections of life, or life as it should be.

The green buzzer buzzed and flashed its clumsy signal to the next patient. An ape of a man lifted himself up slowly and with arduous tread, moved towards the doctor's door.

'What seems to be the problem?'

'I am indescribably ugly and repellent,' said the Apeman.

The doctor looked shocked. 'Do you realise how busy I am? There are patients out there who need my help and limited time. Since when has ugliness been a medical disorder?'

'It is a disorder of my limbs and it is ruining my life.'

'Well, I am afraid that you will have to accept the judgement of your Maker.'

'So you didn't make me, then?' cried the Apeman.

'No, but I did,' said God and, showing the infinite pity in his soul, stretched down his hands and remoulded the Apeman into Adonis. The doctor looked on unsurprised: 'Well, that would appear to settle that! Next time, young man, I expect at least a hernia, gallstones or a really nasty skin complaint.'

The beautiful and bright edition of the male hominid arose, glared from dark blue eyes into the void searching for his reflection, and seemed to suck all life into his vigorous chest. He grasped the door as though it had been insolent in being shut to him, and threw it open with the force of a Greek hero. A paraplegic who, by chance, had at the very same time tentatively placed his prematurely shrunken hand around the handle on the opposite side, was sprawled headlong into the room, at the feet of the princely person. Then the gallant and godlike warrior against the decrepit nature of the mass, set his jaw and seized the cripple's crutches with his heavy fist, and set about the destruction of its owner's feeble flanks. With systematic blows to the left and right he made the hewn human scream.

God wept and said: 'See how my interventions are interpreted. I assist the stricken and the stricken strikes and wreaks havoc.'

'Why do you crucify these frail limbs? Have you no pity in your soul?' called the cripple. The paladin of the powerful continued to punish humanity that does not conform, and then went off in search of his own reflection.

So what is the meaning of this parable? It is that you should be wary of those who claim to have God on their side. They can be cruel. Equally, one should distrust the unshakeable men who know how we are made, and cannot believe. Their advice is dangerous to those who feel. God is not so powerful that he can banish badness, but he is more powerful than those who would be gods.

Of course, you might prefer a more secular exegesis. It could be that when people are freed from some particular oppression they turn out to be more cruel than their former oppressors. Others might argue that the point is that beauty has become the obsession of our age – the hierarchy up which we all try to scramble, kicking others in the teeth as we do so. More prosaically, it may simply be the case that doctors are the new priests and going to the doctor is one hell of a pain in the crotch.

And what is the point of a parable that is followed by the author's gloss? The point is that I am a stunted poet. From the well of words we must draw what is well-shaped, but is not commonplace. This is not necessarily the truth, nor indeed a truth.

Reader, you may also be sceptical about my story, you may consider me some bizarre and twisted intellect that has cobbled together various ill-matching fictional elements. Put your mind at ease – a detailed structural analysis of the text will prove the truth of my tale.

Once upon a time, in the land of Russia, where even shopping lists have profound philosophical significance, there lived a learned professor. After many years of dedicated study, he discovered that all the works of fiction that had ever existed, whether written or oral, had something in common; shall we call it the arcane common denominator of human fantasy that goes back to our prehistory, who knows, perhaps back to some garden of Eden where God's human prototypes discussed the arguments for and against eating the forbidden fruit, at a time when the market still hadn't been swamped by the insipid Golden Delicious? The professor discovered that the beginning of all stories was, without exception, to be found at the beginning, and the end was always to be found at the end. He also discovered that the middle was in practically all cases to be found somewhere between the beginning and the end. Now I realise that put like that, in layman's language, it is difficult to grasp the full meaning of what he had discovered, but the greatness of any new concept is not to be found so much in its content as in the way it is conveyed.

The learned academic said let the beginning be A, the end be C and the middle be B. He applied this scheme to many thousands of statistically representative stories and found the order ABC was maintained in a convincing 100% of the sample taken. By this algebraic analysis, he also laid down a scientific foundation for literary criticism in the future, and I am sure that none of us would want to argue with his findings.

Now let us consider my story and you will immediately notice that the end of my metamorphoses is in the middle and now my journey in human form is about to begin, also in the middle. Furthermore the middle is at the beginning and at the end, in that I begin and end my tale in a state of existential dismay, although it is true that at the end my dismay is due to experience, while at the beginning it is due to inexperience. In other words, reader, or more precisely in other letters, this book may be represented by the formula BCAB; ergo it is not a work of fiction.

Have you ever considered the power that these fiction-writers have? They have total power over their own fantasies, they can create and destroy, they can drive their creations to tragic ends or happy eternities, they can travel through time and space, and they don't even need to respect the rules of the physical world we live in. But on the other hand, there could be some limits to that freedom. They probably live in fear of the critics, they must deliver a story that is different enough to earn the crown of originality, but not so different that no-one knows how to read it (although the genius of this dying century has been to transcend this rule, and the elect have been able to achieve greatness through obscurantism unrivalled since scholasticism). Writers must always have some nit-picking critic in their fantasy who points at each passage and says, 'that is awkward, that is too long and repetitive, that will open you to ridicule, that is too ornate, that is childishly plain,' and with each comment these poor writers will find the scope of their sovereignty limited until they are little more than constitutional monarchs, and far from the demiurges they would wish to be.

I have lived my life as though it were a book to be written, and often I can barely distinguish fact from fiction. Recently I was invited to a fancy dress party and I went as a policeman. While I was returning home I decided to arrest one of my fellow revellers for being drunk and disorderly. I took him to the station, and being a determined member of the naturalist school, I pitilessly twisted his arm into a half-nelson, but as soon as I got there, I was the one to be arrested both for being drunk and disorderly and for impersonating a public official. This, I think, is fairly typical of my life; I have always been punished for both my reality and my fantasy.

If I were to write a work of fiction, I would write for a purpose, not for any aesthetic ideal, but to hit where it hurts, to insult and to disturb. But how do you write in an era in which everyone shouts and nobody listens, in an era in which every superlative sounds as alarming as the dripping of the tap, and only heightens our desire for total silence, for the void of a material existence of sublime unconsciousness. If I were to write in fables, using some silly symbolic code, you might throw my book down in anger and cry: 'What is this mystification? Speak as you wish to be heard and not in riddles. I haven't time for riddles. Riddles are for intellectual poseurs, those who wrap up their poverty of thought in the coloured patterns of childish dreams.'

But perhaps you like childish dreams because they amuse you, and why not? The first purpose of every statement is to amuse in one way or another, for otherwise it would not survive. This is one of nature's cruellest laws: the survival of the fittest permutations of words. But true to my perverse character, I might suddenly try, halfway through the novel, to change style in the absurdly illogical attempt to appease those who have already thrown the book away. I might start to propound, to claim, to suggest, to hold forth at length on those big issues that somehow shrink to absurdity whenever you mention them. This is the kind of stuff that likes to dress up in the gaudy clothes of mystery and symbolism, the kind of stuff that laughs at plain-speaking men.

A professor called me into his study to give me his advice. He sat massively in a leather-bound armchair that sat within a roomful of leather-bound learning and tastefully arranged *objets d'art.* He arranged his smile to match his aesthetically agreeable surroundings and gave his judication: 'Okay – maybe you can do something with fables these days. Magical realism and all that. But, frankly, dialogues are dull – they have nothing to say to the modern age'. But what he could not understand is that those who spew out words from rough and irregular odysseys of failure can only write as they know how and not to satisfy the academician. Those of you who, like the professor, think that structure and genre must respect certain rules should throw the book down now. Those of you with stronger digestion, read on!

I must explain some quirks of mine. If I cook a meal, I am always tempted to throw in every ingredient in my greedy desire to own every taste by using it. Very often the various conflicting flavours cancel each other out, creating insipidness from excess. If I travel to an unknown town, I try to avoid walking down the same street twice. I never move in a straight line, always in circle. This means that I discover many places without fully understanding their relative positions in the town: I achieve a state of enlightened confusion.

Our English language has branches weighed down with the heavy dew of set phrases, literary references, worn-out words, dead metaphors, grey hyperboles and expressions of feeling which lost all feeling when our culture was still young. The clever weave new words around this richness, this over-ripeness, but they do not re-invent feeling; they simply make a great show of their erudition and bravura. Our pens are not dry, but our words are. If only I had a young language, then I could make you weep. Such a trash of words can I spew out and fill the world with half-constructed truths, but find me the words that don't scatter in the wind like autumn leaves.

CHAPTER SEVEN

Egalitarians Anonymous

Hope. Its absurdity and usefulness. The author's beliefs are challenged, and he learns to live with the fragility of ideals.

Spring eternal! Second sister and most human
of the three majuscule maidens,
high-sounding on priest pursed lips,
the trinity of virtue.
Fickle friend and demiurge of dreams,
you help us skyward build the themes
of our collective happiness,
and fill with greater substance
the cold steel coffins of reality.
How hollow sounds the hardness
of all that we can touch;
the folly of your ether will I barter for his coarse clutch
How unreal is your realism,
socialist soldier on the move.
My hand in hers, I will follow for
I do prefer your youthful spirit,
your belief in us or what we could be,
and even your fanatic fight,
to the murder and the greed-gored dismemberment
of our collective corpse,
hard-heralded by the vultures of the Right.

WHERE DO WE PICK up the scent of egalitarianism? We are born in a society riven by class, power and wealth, and we are expected perhaps to consider this the natural order of things. During adolescence we gradually become aware of the vague physiognomy of the society we live in. Primarily it is not the public thing itself but new vocabulary, heavy with the distilled insights and prejudices of past centuries, that conveys to us this initial image. And such a thing as *class*: the word with its many meanings always flies in the face of something that we may and should have felt: that all men and women are equal. The feeling, if not the thought, is almost instinctive, but rarely survives into adulthood, because the instinct towards group or class identity is also strong, even if it is the unadmitted class of those who would destroy class, the self-righteous iconoclasts of the images of wealth, the heroes that unhorse the heroes of the past and would replace them with their own meagre and warted epopoeia. Because we can consider concepts before we properly meet the realities they are built on, political consciousness, which is often little more than blind faith in reason, is in its youthful stages a sentiment of such purity and generosity that it can only evoke irritation and admiration when, once we have passed on to the older generation, we encounter it in emergent youth. The balance between the two conflicting emotions varies according to our politics, but both elements are always present.

I must have had a certain predisposition to the Left when I dreamt of the strange cathedral. The years went past. I cannot tell you how many were in my metamorphosed form. I ceased to be a punk. I worked in a record shop in my home town of Croydon. I became, if it doesn't sound too immodest, something of an expert in pop music of the Eighties and the Nineties. After some time, I decided to investigate this business of animals and human beings, given my own very specialist experience of having been cramped into the restricted forms of two quadrupeds and two species of bird.

I went to visit a great man of the Left. 'Have a drink,' he said and proceeded to pour brown pleasant-smelling liquid into two unmatching glasses. 'Bowmore,' he declared, knowing that I wouldn't recognise the name and identifying himself as a man who, amongst all his other political and cultural interests, cared about whiskies. He was tall, sinewy, but not quite thin. His accent was a northern English variety of standard. His face was generally sombre but given to sudden moments of animation. In particular, just after the ponderous elaboration of some thought, he would glance at you sharply and smile with disarming expectation. You felt that dialogue for him was a very important thing, the moment when he truly became himself. There was something of the eagle about him.

'You've asked,' he said, 'in what ways humans differ from animals or, shall we say, from the other animals. Common arguments have been our use of language and the fact that we alone are supposed to be aware of the inevitability of our death. An interesting one, that last idea, because people nowadays – that is affluent people of the West – live their lives as though they really were going to go on living forever.'

'You mean jogging and health fanaticism?' I prompted.

'Well, partly. That's more of a by-product. The fear of anything that undermines that illusion of eternal life, such as the whiff of someone else's cigarette or the slightest drop of cholesterol-laden butter in your diet. The line between sensible behaviour and the obsessive has become blurred. But then again, people were probably always obsessed with their health. No, the problem is that even with the twenty years or so of extra life provided by modern medical science and a national health service, life is still a short affair. And now we live it as though it wasn't. Childhood is primarily for fun, self-expression and the total absence of a frustrated will. We enter adulthood later, far too late. We spend the next twenty years changing partners and being obsessed about our emotional life. We are like disgruntled shoppers trying on so many different clothes that we forget why we originally came into the store. No-one lives up to the ideals suggested by cinema and ads. Then and only then do we choose to take up some totally inappropriate pastime for the run-up to middle age – such as playing the violin or becoming a ballet dancer.'

'Sounds okay to me,' I said. 'You're not telling me that Victorian discipline should be re-imposed on children, with a few of them shoved up chimneys for good measure? Or that a few talented ones should be plucked Soviet-style from their parents and hot-housed until eighteen to become the opera singers and ice skaters of tomorrow?'

'Of course not,' replied the sage, 'I'm not calling for the return of the rod. The more we can extend life, improve its quality and expand leisure, the better. But imagine for a moment that we really could live forever. Would we learn a foreign language or climb a mountain, "because it's there"? Why bother when we can do it later in one of the many, the endless decades that stretch out before us? Have you noticed how people live in a large, exciting and cosmopolitan city? They rarely bother to visit its museums, galleries, theatres, beautiful buildings and pleasant squares. Why? Because they can do it next week or next month. But if those same people go on holiday to an equally exciting city, they will assiduously frequent all it has to offer, programming it to fit into the limited period of their stay.'

'You're saying that because death appears more distant – is kept more distant, we fail to use our lives properly – to plan them even with its maximum possible span in mind.'

'Exactly,' he said. 'The trick is to live long and leisured lives, but also to feel the pressures of our limited lifespan.'

'Hold on, you're confusing me here. Leisure and pressure – aren't these contradictory concepts?'

'I'm not explaining myself well, and indeed the question is contradictory,' explained the kindly champion of the Left. 'We are pressured now – very pressured. Stressed, we like to say. We are surrounded by labour-saving devices but have no time. The leisure I refer to is closer to the classical idea of *otium* – that is time to read, reflect, saunter, talk to your neighbour and look emptily into the distance to feel your own smallness. It is time that is productive not in what you make but in what it makes you. We have time, but we spend it watching television, getting drunk, arguing over absurd aspects of our self-obsessed lives and, of course, shopping.'

'So how,' I asked, 'do we get out of this cycle of wasted leisure and pressured living?'

'A few isolated individuals may manage it, but it is not easy. Eventually we will have to abandon our high-growth economies, but I don't see that happening for some time. For the present, we live in the present as individuals and as societies. Medieval societies started to erect buildings that even their grandchildren would never see completed. Now we live more like animals, desperately seeking to fulfil ourselves within the present moment. And the activity that most typifies living solely for the present is consumerism. The moment reaches its own fulfilment immediately, and is attached to no other moment. But as it inevitably proves to be unfulfilling, we paradoxically inhabit a false past of nostalgia and a false future in which consumption will finally conform more closely to the ideal consumer dream. By living totally in the present, we fail to really enjoy it.'

'I like this idea. By living solely in the present like animals, we fail to really experience it.'

'Precisely,' he confirmed with his lively expression radiating across the room, 'by living unconnected to our past and future selves, we lose something of our present reality, just as by living as atomised individuals unconnected to other members of our societies, we lose something of our individuality. But let me take up the point of the other distinction between humanity and animals: that of language. All recent industrial history has been about deskilling. Indeed I would go further: technological advances over the last three thousand years are about linguistic deskilling and greater access to knowledge. First the invention of writing meant that some basic concepts could be retained indefinitely by a society, but it wasn't until the invention of the printing press that society could really start to accumulate knowledge and radically improve its methods of production. Of course, some people will point to other inventions, but I am one of those who believes that without the printing press and the diffusion of knowledge, many of those inventions would not have taken place – or perhaps more importantly, would not have been remembered. The computer and other more recent inventions have carried further this process of mechanised memory and redundant human memory.'

'Dr Johnson,' I said, suddenly grasping at an unexpected straw of erudition, 'claimed that we have two types of knowledge: what we hold in our memories and what we know where to find through the appropriate works of reference.'

'Well done,' the savant smiled, 'that is the point I'm making. The Somali tribes of the Ogaden are not literate, but they can almost universally extemporise oral poetry that is a form of shared memory and a form of individuality at the same time. If we leave aside the massive technical terminology of the modern world, their vocabularies and verbal dexterity is greater than ours, but as a society it is difficult for them to move forward because they have no collective way of accumulating knowledge on a very large scale. My point is that modern man is physically more comfortable, but increasingly deprived linguistically and intellectually. Society's knowledge increases, but the individual's decreases.'

'I'm not convinced.'

'Look around you at all these machines. How many do you understand? Do you know how the phone, fax and motor car work?'

'I can change a sparking plug.'

'Yes, when it probably doesn't have to be changed. And then you call a mechanic.'

'Who also happens to be a human being.'

'Yes, but one who does just that.'

'But I particularly wanted to know how this distinction between man and animal could be applied to politics.'

'You're right,' and he flashed a smile that warmly communicated his expectations from our dialogue. 'Well, the traditional – the classical – approach was to perceive the beehive or the ant-hill as the perfect republic, and this is a very good place to start. The Left is currently attacked from all sides, and indeed some believe it historically defeated. They may be right, but if they are, I think there is little hope for humanity. However, the Left did make one tragic and enormous mistake in the twentieth century – it perceived the ideal human society to be a republic of bees – of identical and industrious workers. By education and example, they believed that a perfectly balanced, educated and above all rational citizen would evolve.'

'To be fair, the Left was not alone in this. All political currents in the twentieth century tended to perceive society as a mass. We can see that in the uniformity of the architecture and dress over the first sixty years of the century.'

'I agree,' he nodded eager to continue with his train of thought, 'but I believe we have to be harder on the Left – we must demand higher standards from it than from other political currents. The Left forgot the importance of the individual and invented silly expressions such as "petty-bourgeois individualism". It forgot that the principal aim of the Left since Winstanley, when the Left as a term did not yet exist, through the American and French revolutions to the Chartists, has been democracy – that ultimate act of individualism whereby the individual makes a political decision in the total privacy of the polling booth, and not even his or her spouse or best friend need know or be sure what that political decision was. We may say that current democracies are imperfect. In America, it is a rich man's game and no parties of the Left can stand. In Europe, things are moving in that direction. But the problem is not to restrict democracy but to extend it.'

'Marx didn't say very much – in fact he should have said more about the nature of socialist society.'

'Hold on. We shouldn't get hung up of what any individual did or did not say.'

'Okay,' I conceded, trying to pick up my point, 'but what I wanted to say is that in his comments on the Paris Commune, Marx made it clear that socialism was about very extensive democracy. All national assembly members and elected officials – there were to be many of these – had to be recallable on demand and could not earn more than the average worker's salary. Why then did it go so wrong? How come people who call themselves Marxists and Communists ended up pouring so much scorn on democracy.'

'Two reasons principally,' he said more solemnly. 'They are related but one is in the nature of the thing and the other is how the thing turned out by accident of history. The first is that people who believe strongly in anything, believe that they know best. For instance, they may argue that democracy cannot work when not everybody is literate and free from superstition. They have to be educated or even taught to think in a particular way, and only then can they be given the responsibility of taking decisions. We are talking here of where utopianism slips towards fanaticism. The second reason is that the Russian Revolution and Lenin's leadership pushed this tendency much further than anyone would have imagined – in fact to a point where fanaticism led to an inability to perceive reality. Before Lenin's rise to power, a Russian writer defined Marxists of his kind as "misanthropes entertaining their own fantasies". Lenin failed to understand that the proletariat did not want a dictatorship in its name, it wanted greater freedoms. It did not want to be a mass; it wanted the right to enjoy its individuality. Even the three things he promised: peace, bread and land, were not given or given only briefly. And yet the soldiers who died in the Civil War defending their revolution were not dying for the gulag, forced collectivisation and an end to all free political debate – they were dying for some egalitarian ideal, however vague, and some ideal of freedom, however limited.'

'So the virtuous human republic is not a republic of worker bees, but a republic of individuals.'

'That is right, and here's another paradox. Some people think that egalitarian societies are regimented and uniform. If you are talking about societies with very limited economic resources, they are right to some extent, because the distribution of wealth means that everyone has a shirt if not necessarily a shirt of their own choice. In those economic conditions, this is both right and sensible, even though right-wingers would accuse it of being grey and uninteresting. Hence, they find Battista's Cuba and its lack of freedoms acceptable and even exciting. A place of fun, prostitutes and gambling. But they find Castro's Cuba with its better housing, education system and health service to be an insult to their "liberal values". Liberal values, I should add, that are only slightly stirred, if at all, by the horrendous crimes of someone like Pinochet. As the economic resources of a country increase, it can provide diversity even as an egalitarian society – indeed, I would go further and say that only an egalitarian society can really provide diversity and individualism.'

'Because the economies of scale mean that we are increasingly faced with a consumer choice between almost identical products that differ only in their packaging,' I picked up his point. 'So that's it then – we just have to persuade the Blairs and Schroeders of this world to go back to good old social-democracy that redistributes wealth, subsidises cultural diversity, educates us and keeps us healthy. I can go along with that.'

'Yes, social-democracy looks better with every passing year, as the utilitarians and free-marketeers chip away at it. But it is still a model based on high-growth economies – which is fine in a way, if our little planet could stand it. Let me bring you to another distinction between humans and animals that was pointed out by Sartre. Humans, he said, are the only things whose existence precedes their essence. The essence of a table exists before it is made, and it is designed to fulfil a particular purpose. The essence of a lion, namely a predatory animal that exploits a very specific environmental niche and behaves in a particular manner, is there before it is born and it is more or less forced to conform with that essence. A human being is, according to Sartre, free to invent his or her own essence. You could add that modern technology has created even greater choice, even though many people are incapable of availing themselves of it. What we need therefore is a society that makes it easier for people to develop their individuality.'

'Which you have said is an egalitarian society that interferes in the market to create diversity, particularly cultural diversity.'

'Yes,' he said, 'but the problem of the high-growth economy, which is exhausting this little planet of ours is that all the necessities of life, such as housing, clothing and food are very expensive, while luxuries are relatively cheap. This means poverty for those on low incomes. Above a certain level people can live like kings, if they weren't so frightened of falling below it. If you travelled in Eastern Europe before the fall of the Berlin Wall, you realised that you were in a conformist, illiberal and even claustrophobic society, but it did have one advantage: those necessities were very cheap. Indeed the problem was one of supply of luxury goods given the disposable income created by the low cost of housing, clothing and food. A society that could combine the low-growth economy, the cheap provision of necessities and the highest degree of political and civil liberties would be a society capable of defending its environment, reducing the stress of a highly neurotic society and giving its citizens the maximum ability to be their own distinctive and original selves.'

'Ah, utopia. How sweet the dream.'

Perhaps slightly offended, he looked at me for a second and then smiled. 'Yes, the dream is sweet, but it does not reflect any real optimism on my part. I am deeply pessimistic. People think that society has no choice but to follow its current headlong course. We must learn to dream a little more, or reality will prove impractical.'

'Well, here we have something peculiarly human – we're back to our sense of future,' I mused. 'We humans dream, plan and invent. We decide how best things should be not only for ourselves but for everyone else. Where does the dreamer become the megalomaniac? You're contradicting yourself. Which is it: optimist or pessimist?'

'People are constantly arguing over this one. Some say that to be anything but pessimistic is to be criminally complacent. So many things can go wrong in life, and the greater the responsibilities the greater should be the prudence inspired by a healthy dose of pessimism. Others claim that pessimism leads to an inability to perceive a better future and therefore to work towards it, even if it will probably prove impossible to go all the way. I resolve this problem with my own little formula: hope for everything and expect nothing.'

'Hope for everything and expect nothing – yes, very formulaic ...'

He interrupted me, and this time he really did look offended. 'Look, I agreed to talk to you, because I find your question interesting, but I am a busy man ...'

'No, no, don't get me wrong. I like it – "hope for everything and expect nothing" – it has a good sound to it and a lot of good sense too, I think. It's simply that my reaction is much more emotional. I am pessimistic because I cannot see how I could be anything else. Perhaps I could have been optimistic, if I had been born ten years earlier and belonged to the generation that protested over Vietnam. But then all the problems for humanity seem to stack up. Third World debt caused disruption in countries that were renamed "developing" in a wilful act of spin to cover their rapacious exploitation. The population spirals. The ecological problems look terrifying. The West goes down the road of the "flexible" economy, which means everybody thinks they're going to lose their job next week. Nasty, brutal and criminally stupid wars have come out like a rash. And on top of that, even if we solved all those terrible problems, it would take just one psychopath – and there are a few around – to set off one of the proliferating nuclear bombs, and half the planet would be unusable. How can anyone of my generation be optimistic?'

'You're right. Optimism has nothing very logical about it. It can be dangerous, if it becomes the dominant approach. It is more an act of faith required to stop us from becoming politically inactive. If we all go off to mind our gardens like Candide, then the world really would have no hope, not only of improving but even of surviving. There has to be that moment of dreaming, that creative moment that perceives possibilities. I say "possibilities", and that's important. If the possibilities become certainties, then you have become a very dangerous person, a fanatic, and it really would have been better if you'd stayed at home to mind your garden.'

'But what can we really do?' I asked. 'Before you encourage people to abandon the pleasantness of their gardens, shouldn't you at least explain how they can change things? Even in democracies, it seems difficult to impose any kind of popular will. I've heard that around 70 per cent of Americans would like some form of national health system, but the wealthy taxpayers and the insurance companies would never allow it.'

'They would if the issue became important enough to the American people – if they started to believe that they could change it. Every society has its own pain threshold. It will not allow things to go past a certain point. Even medieval society would finally stir and say, no, I won't accept this – I won't accept a poll tax, I won't accept these rents, I won't accept this level of military service. Then it would thrash about ineffectually, but enough to frighten the powerful into partial retreat. The pain threshold then was very high, and now it is much lower. The powerful prod the beast more gingerly and are always ready to run away.'

'Only by becoming powerful can you have any hope of changing things for the better.'

'Only certain kinds of men and women become powerful,' said the learned man. 'They are the arrogant. I cannot abide the arrogant. I feel no envy for the arrogant and the powerful, I feel only contempt. I no longer even get angry at their lack of principle, their lack of self-awareness, their greed, their shallowness, their pomposity and their outrageous sense of moral superiority. When one of them, surprisingly and uncharacteristically, acts in a principled manner, I rejoice. All that intellectuals – men and women of ideas – can hope to do is nudge the powerful, prick their conscience a little bit. But they shouldn't get their hopes up. Power is a magnet to power – not to ideas.'

'Wouldn't it be sensible to play the power game – and play it as dirty as you like – and once you have attained a position of power, implement changes to ...'

'To establish the virtuous republic,' he finished the sentence for me. 'This is Machiavelli's idea. He was, in spite of the various interpretations that have been put on his work, a great moralist. He called on princes to establish virtuous republics rather than dynasties. He thought it better to defeat political enemies with deceits than in open warfare which is destructive and of uncertain outcome. Hence the end justifies the means, although he never actually used these words. But in one short passage of his *Discourses* he undermines his entire life's work. Power can only be achieved by evil means. Only by the exercise of power can good be implemented on a large scale. What is required is a good man who uses evil means, and once established returns to his true and virtuous self. But in this passage, Machiavelli despairingly admits that it is very unlikely that such a man could ever exist. You could add that even if one did, the exercise of the immoral acts required to achieve power even in a democracy would corrupt the individual concerned. The merit of democracy is that it provides for alternation and a degree of control, however tenuous. But power is always power.'

'So what is to be done?' I asked.

'Don't get me wrong. I'm not promoting some form of anarchistic denial of the powerful. They have a role. The fact that as human beings they are relatively unpleasant does not remove the fact that any imposition of order is better than the failure to impose any order at all. We are faced with Hobbes' fundamental assertion that without a state everyone would be at war with everyone. I don't share his very low opinion of humanity as a whole, but he is right in that even a very small amount of vicious people would be enough to cause the complete destruction of all labour, all planning, all that makes human beings different from animals. Inevitably some new form of order always appears.'

'The state is a necessity?'

'I cannot see past the state. I cannot see that far down the road. I am not that much of a utopian. Indeed I would even say that I like the state, or rather I have a kind of love-hate relationship with it. I liked it when the railways belonged to the state. I felt part of them or any other state enterprise. The state does some things very well. Particularly anything to do with forms of insurance, such as national health, pensions, coverage of industrial accidents. It is not just the economies of scale, it is an actuarial reality. But not only this – take the public square for instance, owned as it is by everybody. It is where all citizens come together as equals – it is where the individual and the society meet. You can tell a lot about a country if you observe their public buildings and how they maintain them. In them, you catch a glimpse of the ideal state, which contrasts with the state of inevitably imperfect laws and the arrogant politicians we have spoken of.'

'You can have little love for this government, then.'

'Little indeed', he said. 'They really are like the pigs in 1984 that wear the farmers clothes and smoke his cigars. They can get away with it, because the pain threshold has gone back up a bit. No-one sees any alternative. You see the importance of dreaming. Everyone has stopped dreaming, and they allow these charlatans to pose as champions of the people. They run a *nomenklatura*, a network of patronage, possibly greater than that of their predecessors. They cut back on hard-won rights, while affecting a reforming spirit. They are in many ways like Mussolini, not obviously in that they want to impose a dictatorship, but in a very specific area of their political personality. They support privilege, but claim that the establishment is against them. They wear the clothes of both conservatism and popular radicalism. Jack Straw wishes to do away with the automatic right to juries, an idea like many others that was attacked by New Labour when proposed by their predecessors, and he accuses those who now challenge the idea of being "BMW-driving civil-liberties lawyers". He bolsters the establishment and affects to be against it, or even to be its victim. Their intellectual dishonesty has no limits.'

'And the government,' I joined in, now getting the bit between my teeth, 'quite rightly cold-shoulders a racist like Haider, and then engages in equally racist remarks and humiliates the handful of political refugees this country takes in by providing them with food vouchers or threatening to remove their children.'

'Third-wayism always takes on this form. It runs with the fox and hunts with the hounds. It is dishonesty and obscurantism, and for an intellectual these are cardinal sins.'

'It is hypocrisy and cant, and for an inexpert citizen like myself, these are also cardinal sins,' I added.

'They lack what I call a republican morality, which does exist in some luckier countries. This is blindingly clear in the pathetic way they have approached the reform of the House of Lords. They are a disaster.'

And so we spent many a long hour happily denouncing our government. Now dreaming and now terrified by the unstoppable awfulness of it. We minded the gardens of our minds.

CHAPTER EIGHT

Beyond the Absence of Good and Evil

Charity. The author, perhaps motivated by his increasing years, retraces his steps, tries to understand the past and discusses it all with an enlightened reverend, reverend philosophe or possibly just a man.

To You the smoothing swarm of years,
close-shadowed by that finite end,
have turned my thoughts, my heart perhaps,
but not my faith.
Will that the sagging spring of life bring on?
to follow in the feet of fears
so natural to our unnatured state.
You softened the sorrow,
when I did fret within the frigid frame
of this 'I', this 'my', this 'me' that restless turns
and paces the grey-celled cell that is my brain,
the reason for my reason that reason spurns.

TO AVOID TRAFFIC one day on my way to the shop, I went through some housing estates and then I saw it. I saw the church with the bell-less bell-tower. Only it had a bell. It also had a blue notice-board with golden lettering that said 'Holy Trinity Church – Church of England', and then various information on the vicar and the hours of worship. Fascinated, I decided to go in. There was no-one about, so I continued round to the vicarage and knocked on the door. A man answered. He was a stocky, cherubic figure. In some ways he reminded me of Bacchus, but the overall effect was entirely different, because his eyes sparkled with intelligence and real, not affected, humour. I remember thinking how a slight somatic difference can change the whole tone of a human presence – in this case to an intellectual energy and hospitality that promised an interesting encounter. There was something of the owl about him.

'Are you the vicar?' I asked and the man replied with a bemused curiosity that suggested 'Do I look like a vicar?'

'No, I'm the vicar's brother. If you're looking for the vicar, I'm afraid he's not in.'

'Well, I wasn't looking for anyone in particular. I have a sort of theological question. I was thinking about this business of being saved. Is it only humans that can be saved, or does salvation also include dogs, cats, rattlesnakes, shrimps and one-cell creatures that busy around in primeval swamps trying to sort out their DNA?'

'I don't think you're a believer yourself?' he asked.

'No, not really.'

'Then maybe it was divine intervention that got me to answer the door, instead of my brother. I'm just visiting, you see – but he wouldn't have given you any coherent answer at all, and he would only have tried to convert you. Such a tiresome and pointless business, this proselytising – and nowadays there seem to be fewer ideas and more proselytisers.' He beckoned me in and added impishly, 'I'll get some tea brought in.' We went through to a room that was slightly dank, old-fashioned in its decor and well-worn in its dusty furnishings. A kind of genteel poverty with the odd touch of kitsch. The man turned up one of those electric fires that are badly disguised as coal fires, and then threw himself back playfully into an armchair while inviting me with a sweep of his arm to take the other one. 'I'm going to really enjoy playing the vicar for a little while', he said as he lifted a bell and rang it. Shortly afterwards a woman came in with a face like a question mark.

'We have a visitor. I wonder if you could bring some tea and biscuits for two?'

The woman looked slightly put out, but after a moment's reflection, appeared to accept the request and disappeared. The man looked overjoyed, as though to say, this is getting better and better. 'Now, my son, what can I do for you?' he said in a mock-vicarly kind of way and then hooted with laughter. 'You must excuse me. I must take this more seriously.'

'No, no. I should be excusing myself. It's a bit of an odd question. To be honest with you, I thought I recognised the church, and I ...'

'Dear boy, don't apologise,' he said expansively. 'I'm thoroughly enjoying myself, although my brother will kill me when he finds out. Now, let's look at the question. All these animals, including ourselves, and no really discrete distinction whereby you can say these ones go to heaven and these ones don't, because a heaven that had amoebas and shrimps would be no kind of heaven at all. You could, I suppose, have the odd cat or dog, if you're that sentimental kind of person. I'm afraid you've got me on a slightly sticky wicket here, my boy.'

'Oh. Why's that?'

'Well, I don't really believe in salvation at all.'

'Ah. So you're an atheist,' I said.

'Did I say that?

'No, but ...'

'No buts about it, young man. Not believing in salvation or even in life after death does not necessarily mean that you don't believe in God.'

'So you do believe in God, but not in salvation?'

'There you go again – jumping to conclusions. I neither believe in God nor disbelieve in Him. I wouldn't be that superstitious.'

'But surely the onus of proof is on those who believe in him. It isn't superstitious not to believe in God.'

'Well, it's not the kind of thing you can really provide much proof about,' said the mock vicar. 'Although I like riling both believers in God and believers in the absence of God, I agree with you that the superstition of the former is greater than that of the latter. The former are dangerously deluded, but the latter do display an unhealthy lack of imagination. Let me put to you a question. Even if God does not exist, isn't it a God-like gift to be?'

'What does that mean?' I asked, beginning to think that this experience might not be very pleasant after all.

'Alright, alright. We don't express ourselves like that. That is not good manners. Let me put it this way. Here we are, these little self-reproducing machines in some obscure corner of a bizarre and ever-increasing universe, and we have within us a sense of being that goes far beyond anything that could be invented by survival of the fittest. Darwin came up with an excellent working hypothesis, I'll grant you – particularly if you consider what they believed in beforehand, but he has hardly answered all the questions, and certainly not the most interesting ones.'

The door swung open brusquely, and with a sigh the woman hurried into the room with a tray of tea and biscuits. She settled it on a small table and starchily asked if we needed anything else. He waited for her to close the door before returning to his argument. 'Take what has just happened.'

'What is that?'

'Well, not very much but also a great deal. You see my brother's housekeeper does not like me very much. I have no idea why, but I'm quite willing to accept that I can be a very irritating person. She has just carried out the very simple process of making a pot of tea and shoving a few biscuits on a tray. But it has become a drama. She is thinking, constantly thinking "Who is that man? What are they talking about?" She is upset. She, at the centre of her own, and to her, extremely important existence, is all in a whirl about who is drinking the vicar's tea.'

'So?'

'Well, think of the tragi-comic grandeur of it. She, who is as complex a pattern of emotions and consciousness as any other human being on the planet, is not thinking about her smallness, her death, her salvation, global warming, genetic engineering or any other major issue. She is worrying about a couple of tea bags because she is protective towards my brother who she sees me as exploiting.'

I shifted in my chair, unimpressed by his arguments, and took a swig of tea made with the disputed tea bags.

'I can see that you're not following me here at all. What I'm saying is that you have to admit to a sense of wonderment, bewilderment and inappropriateness about life. Like suddenly realising that you've come to the wrong party.'

'Look,' I was getting a little irritated, 'what you're saying is that you're an agnostic, a don't know, someone who can't make up his mind, and I can. I'm an atheist and I know it.'

'Okay, so we've established that you belong to the majority religion.'

'Majority religion? That's ridiculous.'

'Well that's what it is nowadays – most people think like you. Or should I say most believers think like you, because most people have always been what you call don't knows, and a very honourable position it is too. Why pretend to know what you cannot possibly know? People think that everybody was a fanatical believer in the Middle Ages – I think they're wrong. Scepticism has always been the most sensible approach and the one most people instinctively follow, even though they often don't like to admit to it, because societies have more set opinions. Once you had to pretend to believe in an absurdly precise set of dogmas, now you have to pretend to be a rigid atheist, or renounce any claim to rational thought.'

'I'm the atheist and you're the agnostic,' I asserted. 'First you say there are more of me, and then you say there are more of you. Make up your mind.'

'Of those with fixed ideas, there are more of you. Of the whole population, there are more of me, particularly if you think that many of those who go around saying they believe something absolutely, still, in the quiet of their more thoughtful moments, probably do experience doubts. If not, I question whether they are still really living and breathing. But anyway I want to challenge your definition of me as an agnostic. I'm a Christian.'

'That's ridiculous. How can you say that you are a Christian, when you are not even sure if you believe in God.'

'Well I've already told you that even Christians who believe or pretend to believe in every letter of the sacred scriptures must have their doubts about the existence of God. It therefore seems only reasonable for a Christian like myself not to believe in the Virgin Birth, the Resurrection, the divinity of Christ or the physical reality of the miracles.'

'That's ridiculous. You can't call yourself a Christian, and then simply discard ninety per cent of what the religion is.'

'My brother would agree with you. He says you have to believe every letter of the Bible or it is all lies – I have no time for such inanities. A friend to whom, like you, I explained my views, looked at me and said "but that's just humanism". Now I'm not one to waste time over definitions, but it strikes me that humanism is about an intellectual break with all previous religion – a kind of 1789 approach to the celestial constitution. I prefer an approach involving historical continuity. Not only is Christianity and its stories an integral part of our last two millennia in Europe and parts of Africa and the Middle East, it was a revolution in human history. Its universality – its inclusion of all races and all castes from nobles to soldiers to slaves – was entirely subversive. If you read a book by Apuleius on a man who was changed into a donkey, you'll find that he referred contemptuously to Christianity as the slave religion, very much as Nietzsche nearly two millennia later referred to it as a herd religion. D'Annunzio, too, referred with similar contempt to smelly proles and socialists in his books, although unlike Apuleius he lacked a sense of humour.'

The reference to metamorphosis made me blush. Did he know something? How could he possibly know? Had my metamorphoses left some mark that an extremely observant mind could somehow detect? Instinctively, I looked down to check that my flies were done up, and then at my feet for no particular reason. There was something very unrelaxing about this conversation. 'I still don't see why you have to define yourself as a Christian, just because you recognise the historical importance of Christianity in the development of Western society.'

'Well, in part it is because it is the only sensible way to be a Christian,' he said. 'It seems abundantly clear to me that most of what science has discovered is incontrovertible fact, and the small part that is not true is simply because they've made a mistake and haven't seen the whole picture, as with the centuries-long dispute over whether light moves in particles or waves. To believe in the literal truth of the Bible, leaving aside the undoubted corruption of the text, is an act of wilful stupidity. I say wilful, because I don't mean that all believers are fools – sometimes they choose to be stupid in very intelligent ways. On the other hand, science is very limited in what it can do. Many of the most interesting things cannot be measured. Hence we are thrown back into the region of doubt. You may think that this is unimportant, but it is not. We face dangers from religious fanatics, but we also face dangers from scientific over-simplification and pseudo-sciences.'

'Like sociology, which someone called "the painful elaboration of the obvious"?'

'Absolutely: the closer you get to human society, the more pernicious pseudo-science becomes. And this is where the collective wisdom and confusion of our literatures and religions come into play.'

'So you're a sceptical Christian?'

'I am indeed. But in a way, I am also a sceptical Muslim, Buddhist, Hindu and Jew.'

'Now you really are pulling my chain.'

'No, no,' he protested. 'I'm not trying to be clever at all. I like to think of religion as a mountain, a rounded mountain whose peak is obscured to everyone. All the religions are trying to climb that mountain, but starting from a different position, so the surrounding scenery is different, but the obscured truth is the same. So Christianity is no better or worse than any other religion; it simply happens to be the one that marked the culture I was born into. Hence, I call myself a sceptical and syncretic Christian.'

'I certainly understand why your friend called you a humanist.'

'We're all entitled to our own opinion,' – he looked slightly irritated and drummed his fingers on the ends of the arms of his chair. After a little while, he started again: 'You have to understand that religiosity and scientific curiosity are both part of our human nature. We think of them as being in conflict, when they are really both part of us and our own particular instincts. Imagine a colony of ants with some human characteristics. Suppose the ants burrowed away into the brickwork of a house, and one of them had the intelligence to discover that his world of bricks had not been built for ants but by humans for humans, how would that change the everyday way his fellow ants perceived their universe? The discovery would be enormously difficult to perform, it would be his passion and the other ants would have to be sufficiently interested in the result to exonerate him from all other duties. For practical purposes, the ants would be better served by lesser discoveries than that of their cosmologist professor, such as maps of the areas they foraged, information on the safest periods to leave the colony and so on. For the average ant labouring across the gritty red expanses, smooth hard-gloss paintwork and linoleum deserts in search of some sticky crumbs dropped like manna from the heavens, everything would have changed metaphysically and nothing physically. The ant perspective, the view, the feel of the world would be exactly the same. But the inner perception of his antness would have been radically altered: he would be more alive and more unsettled. In the same way, we crawl about this world and have to perceive it from our own dimensions. In that cliché'd moment of human rapture and wonder when we see the sun set over a beautiful countryside, who is it that remembers that it is the world that revolves around the sun? To remember would be to destroy the image of the golden chariot that beats out the rhythm of our life, our world, the centre of our human universe that in that moment we very probably love. The real universe with its infinite possibilities and hypotheses is relegated to the greyest of grey cells right at the back of the brain, submerged by the reality of anthropocentric sensations.'

'Someone told me that the ancients perceived the anthill as the perfect republic,' I said thinking of my previous conversation. 'But the whole point about human beings is that they waste time. They build buildings, magnificent buildings for the particular God they believe in, while most of them are living in hovels. And when they are not praying to gods, they are driven by their curiosity to discover the reality around them, discoveries that for the most part have no practical application. The anthill is the rational and utopian republic, but human beings are irrationally engaged in avoiding their economic interests.'

'Wonderful. You're getting the idea. Wastefulness for the sheer pleasure of it is one of humanity's distinguishing features. Not only do human beings expend enormous energies building a house for a God that may not exist, but they also have to ornament it. They have to ornament themselves. They have to ornament their houses. Even if some Spartan belief forces them not to ornament, then their lack of ornamentation is itself an ornamentation. They are constantly saying "Here I am", "This is how I do things", and in some cases more ambitiously "Only I can do it this way". Religion and science are part of this ornamentation, this busying around over things that have nothing to do with the animal necessities of food, shelter and protection.'

'So religion is something that humans seek out?'

'Exactly: rather than God creating man, it was man that invented God – but that does not either prove or disprove the actual existence of God. The proof of this is to be found in the way God has evolved with human society. Christians speak of their loving and forgiving God, but the God of Genesis was a cruel and unforgiving God who purposefully hardened the pharaoh's heart so that he could display his power.'

'Or the story of Abraham and Isaac,' I said in order to show that I wasn't totally ignorant of the Bible. 'How could any God order a man to kill his son merely to test the strength of his faith?'

'The test of Abraham was no trial of faith, but a trial of Abraham's fickle God. Indeed, what kind of God could order a man to kill his son for the absurd purpose of testing the limits of blind obedience? We are ultimately responsible for our moral dilemmas, which are often unreasonably complex, yet Abraham's seems to us to be childishly simple. A needless death to pave the way to his imagined heaven or to accept that his son was arbiter of his own life. After some vacillation he chose, he made an intellectual leap, stood up to the hostile God created of a hostile world, the expanse of day-hot, night-cold, dusty, mean and meagre earth that held in its grasp the wandering tribes of early consciousness, and made God more human, realised a link that held us all together, the first, elementary step in man's understanding or making of God.'

'But how can you justify this interpretation?' I asked. 'Those who argue that the story shows the importance of faith above all other moral requirements are surely on firmer ground. Abraham is rewarded by God with the promise that his seed would prosper into a countless people and inhabit the cities of others.'

'So it would seem,' explained my new-found guru. 'God desists from encouraging murder only to inspire the cuckoo instinct in Abraham's people. Abraham was no saviour; his realisation of a nationalist consciousness is not an example to follow, it is an episode in the struggle to create God in the image of all humanity. The culmination of this struggle was the arrival of Christ, who was divine, not for any miraculous conception, but for his conception of humankind and God.'

'Now that achievement has been made, now the value of every life has been established, do we need the sacred texts? Isn't the march of this democratic age related at least in part to the progressive liberation from religious superstition? Isn't religion just so much useless ballast, no longer required for the next part of civilisation's journey?'

'We constantly have to jettison the refuse of the past to keep ourselves afloat,' he replied. 'However, we must not deny history's collective intelligence. Intellectual production, just like material production, produces its useless by-products; tradition can build up like slag, an unstable material that can smother the present in its viscous cold lava. We tend to veer between the extremes of traditionalism and iconoclasm. Sometimes we arrogantly claim to reinvent all knowledge from the privileged perspective of some contemporary revelation and sometimes we prostrate ourselves before the past. Both extremes are born of our craving for certainties, our instinctive fear of freedom. Very few can find the right balance between the past and present, because it requires an intellectual freedom that few societies encourage.'

'We have established that man is a more turbulent animal than any other. We might now ask whether the modern materialist interpretation makes a clearer distinction between man and beast than when we were all supposed to believe in the holy scriptures.'

'Modern science has shown how we are closely related to the animal kingdom,' he argued. 'It has also reduced us in size relative to the cosmos. It has humbled us to some extent. But at the same time, it has made us more confident of our superiority. It has made us more not less anthropocentric, although the style has changed considerably. People now feel that they have domesticated their world – that they therefore own it and can do with it what they like. To understand the world, we need to discover a new spirituality.'

'It seems to me that spirituality is a word loaded with the empty space of the heavens, a vacuum of meaning.'

'It would for you, for it can never be measured.'

'You will have to do better than that.'

'But this is like that much-ridiculed question "What is the meaning of that painting or that music?" Spirituality, at least in a positive interpretation of the word, is the ability to read part of the message of life, the part that cannot be explained or communicated, except perhaps by art. It is not to be confused with religiosity; atheists sometimes have a certain spiritual sensitivity, while believers can lack it and religious fanatics are precluded from it.'

'You're still being very vague,' I insisted.

'It is a paradox that in a world made small by modern technology, consciousness often extends no further than the prosperous territory of a semi-detached, and at times the immediate vicinity, but only in as much as it affects the mini-kingdom or the Englishman's castle as we proudly call it. Thus the man that is unconcerned about nuclear dumping somewhere else, will be moved to titanic rage by the threat of a high-speed train that at long intervals might send slight tremors through his cabbage patch. That is a lack of spirit in every sense of the word.'

'No, it is simply a lack of solidarity.'

'But what is solidarity, if not a spiritual value?'

'And so you wish to save humanity with a little bit of spiritualism and a little bit of rationalism,' I countered. 'Don't you know how dangerous were the people who knew what was best for humanity in the century that has just passed?'

'I agree that no society, however enlightened, could ever completely educate our selfish passions out of us, and it would be dangerous if it ever tried to ban them by decree. But it is equally wrong to think that we are nothing more than the sum of them – this is of course what Thatcherites believe, and they get very angry with anyone who suggests there is anything more that motivates us. They really believe that we are an ant-hill. Their misplaced idealism disproves their own theory.'

'So they are right that we are motivated by self-interest, but they are wrong to think that we are only motivated by self-interest.'

'The fact that we cannot always control our passions does not mean that we should not attempt to control them, or we end up fulfilling their model,' he explained slightly wearily. 'I do not mean that we should engage in some puritanical crusade, or bigoted concern for public morality; I mean that we must reassert responsibility for ourselves. We may indeed be the Freudian puppets of our childhood environments, the biological dupes of the food we eat and the air we breath or pawns of our lifestyle which in turn may be imposed and beyond our control, but nothing enslaves like the lost belief in our own will caused by too much belief in any of these factors or similar ones. This is not to say that such theories don't have their share of truth: they do indeed limit our freedom, but they should never negate our freedom to struggle for freedom, which in the end is the only freedom that is totally achievable.'

The sounds of his brother the vicar returning could be heard in the hall. My Socratic friend hastened me to the back, and shook my hand warmly as he told me how much he had enjoyed our little chat. I left him the wiser for knowing the breadth of my ignorance and all that Greek stuff. I reflected how much better it is to concentrate on the specific rather than this illusive material. It was good that I have my knowledge of music. It was something you could get hold of. This business of not knowing can be very disconcerting.

CHAPTER NINE

The Dialogue of the Elders

Doubt. The author speaks to several fellow drinkers and receives a bewildering amount of information that he can do nothing with. He finally accepts the business of being a disturbed animal who cannot make any sense of his senses. He communes with nature on a polluted beach.

The frozen form of a past pensively wrought
from cold iron – the heavy hinges creak,
the gate slams shut. And yet I still
would stare upon that tomb of passions
chilled by the wind of change.

Fool! Nothing can be learnt in there.
The skeleton now lacks the flesh –
hopes whose feeble breath was lost
within the marble blast.

It is to warmth and sweet-lipped smiles,
and heady laughter hurled from heavy juices,
to the quickening pace of slower limbs,
and yes, to this drowning earth,
that I must turn the blurred and blunted
conceits of concentration.

A simple thought when neatly told
will defy mass, grow bigger than itself.
The sincere secluded in their truth

and the innocent cry out for words of weight.
We deaden what it is to feel,
so we may make our feelings felt.

I ENTERED. No TV, no music and no flickering betting-machines in the inner gloom of the whitewashed walls. It was not until I had sat down that I realised that the other two people at the table were drunk. One was a woman who reminded me a little of Fotis. Good-looking in spite of the drunkenness that somehow weighed her down like an onerous and unavoidable duty. She swayed and took a little time to focus me in her line of sight, before releasing a flow of words. It was the kind of rant that only drunks can engage in. A circle of thoughts and obsessions that turned around on itself endlessly repeating the causes of its torrential power. The woman was a fairly successful actress working for the BBC in London who was enjoying her holidays away from it all. In spite of her success, the BBC establishment always unnerved her. The main reason for her distress, as revealed by alcoholic lack of inhibition, was the way women in that institution power-dressed and looked down their noses at her. 'They think they're better than you, they think they're so smart just because ... because they've got this fucking poker stuck up their arses.' She stared at me unsteadily as though attempting to understand whether the full force of her argument had had a convincing effect. 'Am I or am I not a good-looking woman? Am I what you would call a good lay?' I was, in truth, able to confirm that I thought she was, although I wasn't quite sure as to how much conviction I should put into the reply. She stared at me in an attempt to assess the honesty of my reply, and then appeared to give up, took her distance, and rambled on although no longer specifically directing her arguments to me. Alone. She was alone, and that loneliness infected me. I shifted on my stool uncomfortably, unsure as to whether I had been dismissed, and neither wishing to appear rude by ignoring a drunk on the one hand or interfering with someone's right to indulge in drunken misery on the other.

Then the man, who didn't appear to have anything to do with the woman, started off on his own drunken trajectory: 'Paranoia is a deep well of loneliness that stretches up above you. Down in there, you cannot see or understand the world, and the sounds you hear are terribly distorted. The only way you can get to the top and see out, is to fill the whole damn thing', and he swung his arm in what was supposed to be a grand gesture, but lost impetus as the arm had been required to keep him upright, 'with drink. That's right, with drink I said, all the way to the bloody top, so that you can see out, of course.' His voiced dropped: 'But then you feel as though you're drowning.'

I was beginning to feel depressed by their drunkenness and my own sobriety. I envied their state, but had no wish at that time of becoming like them. They were too far ahead of me, and by the time I caught them up, they would have been swimming through alcoholic dreams. It was time to go. I was about to move when three men came in and sat down at the table. 'Hello, Angus,' said one, 'are you slightly the worse for wear?'

The drunk, who was a chubby man in his mid-fifties, stared back sullenly: 'I'm quite alright thank you, if it's any of your business.'

The names of the men, as I was to discover during the evening, were Seumas, Donald and Calum. Seumas was a tall athletic man with sharp features and a slightly impatient manner. Donald was short, stocky and laid-back. Calum was of average height with a black beard speckled with grey, and also appeared to be of a relaxed nature. All three men were in their early fifties.

'What are you here for?' asked Calum.

'Just wandering and wondering,' I answered elliptically.

'So what are you wondering about?'

'Well for starters, how do humans distinguish themselves from animals?'

'Ah, is the whisky bottle deep enough and the night long enough for this one?' said Donald, looking at the ceiling in exasperation. 'I feel that we're in for a great deal of pointless blether.'

'Well, we could start with Dostoyevsky,' pronounced Calum, 'who said that man is distinguished from the animals by his ability to curse the world.'

'I like that,' I replied enthusiastically, 'that's a poet's answer. I've spoken to a political thinker and a theologian, and they taxed my little brain with all sorts of stuff. But here's an answer that cuts all the corners and contains much of what they said.'

'And men are all animals. Have you thought of that one?' said the drunken woman. 'We just have to put up with the poor little bastards, I suppose. They must be useful for something, but I can't think what.' The drunken man seemed to take this as a personal insult and had to be restrained by Seumas and Donald. He then strangely had a change of heart, lay down on the bench and peacefully went off to sleep.

'Men are all animals,' she repeated. 'Well, that's my experience.'

The men around the table who were still awake felt that there was probably some truth in this assertion, but didn't know how to react. 'Oh fuck you,' she said, irritated by their silence, and off she went to get another drink.

'The main thing about humans now,' said Seumas with the air of a chairman introducing some committee, 'is that there are so many of us, and we're to be found almost everywhere, running the planet and controlling every other animal.'

Donald smiled to himself before fixing us with mocking sparkling black eyes. 'You think of all those millions upon millions of lives, loves, ambitions and feelings of pain, and you feel numbed by an infinity of intensity. How can so much passion exist? A kind of EC surplus. Not a butter mountain, but a mountain of emotion.'

'Humanity, taken as a whole, has a frightening dimension. Each individual in the six-billion-odd souls who inhabit this planet is both desire and disappointment. One may want a better address in Manhattan and another may want another field to grow more rice. But they are all driven.'

'Seumas, you're confusing quantity with quality,' said Donald quietly, and then more loudly, 'quantity and quality are not the same thing.'

The others looked at him, surprised by the assertiveness with which he stated the obvious. A smile wandered across his pink face, and hovered uncertainly, as though balanced between conflicting forces. 'Quantity and quality?' they prompted.

'That's right: quantity and quality. And one ambition follows another. Did you know an interesting thing?'

'Now what would that be, Donald?'

'In the Twenties, Hitler was so pleased when he became the editor of a right-wing newspaper that he wrote to a friend saying that if only the newspaper kept up its circulation, he would have achieved all his ambitions. Fifteen years later, the world was not big enough for his ambitions. Entire nations were of little consequence. He thought in continents and in peoples to be destroyed. You cannot compare his final ambitions with the ordinary ambitions of a Chinese or Indian peasant to have another field or a piece of agricultural machinery.

You cannot even compare his final ambitions with his early ones, although the latter certainly led to the former with the help of circumstance.'

'Alright Donald,' said Seumas, 'humans are different from animals because they are ambitious. Animals might fight to get to the top of the pack and increase their chances of reproduction, but once they're there, they're quite happy to sit back and enjoy themselves. Humans are restless. There is always another ambition that beckons.'

'That is not all; it is not just a personal thing. Humans are only really happy when unhappily turning things over in their mind with the hope of happy resolution of it all in the future. If we lose that hope of possible future happiness, we become really depressed. That's the best we can hope for, unhappy but hopeful bewilderment in place of clinical depression.'

'That's our Donald,' said Calum, 'always guaranteed to give you a cheery evening.'

Donald continued, enjoying his miserable outlook. 'Man conceitedly calls himself *homo sapiens*, knowing man, to distinguish himself from the animals, but it is precisely when he knows or thinks he knows that he becomes most like an animal, following the routine of his desires. But when he thinks, he ceases to know or to know very much. To distinguish ourselves from the animals we should call ourselves *homo cogitans*, thinking man.'

'We are now consuming man,' said Seumas. 'A totally passive condition. You're right: we think we know a lot, because we use all this complicated equipment: computers, mobile phones, flash cars, and whatever, but we know less than previous generations. We are completely de-skilled, not only in our work, our cooking and the maintenance of our environment, but also in cultural production: our stories, our music, our dance. It all comes from afar. We consume artistic products with the same consciousness of a sheep munching on grass.'

'Come on, come on,' said Calum. 'Give you fellas a few drams and you're away with the fairies. Compared with the past, we are now healthier, we live longer and we have more leisure to be who we are. All this romantic claptrap about the past is the luxury of those who can afford it.'

'Nobody's saying we were better off in the past', said Seumas with impatience of someone who feels he has to explain something that is almost self-evident. 'But we are de-skilled, and so we shouldn't feel so bloody superior. We have swapped one religion for another called materialism. Religions have always been sedatives to relieve the pain of thinking, and therefore not knowing. The answers provided by the modern religion may be more sophisticated but they are also less effective. That's why they have to be bolstered by another drug: continuous and unremitting consumerism.'

'This is so much crap,' said Donald pugnaciously. 'You can think what you like. Do I care? Does anyone care? But once they did. You couldn't disagree with transubstantiation or they would murder you, but if you crossed a national border, you couldn't agree with it or they would do the same. Don't bore me with the past. You can sit and philosophise – or pontificate – and no-one really cares. You can get on with being your *homo cogitans*, and leave us lesser beings to have a happy time consuming until we suck the planet dry. And by the time that happens neither you nor I will have to bother about it.'

'But Seumas has a point,' said Calum calmly. 'Art is another thing that distinguished humans from animals, and yet now we are completely alienated from its production. Once art was everywhere, part of everyday life. I'm not talking here simply of the classical traditions, but popular art, real art that lives on through its constant re-elaboration. Something of it lives on in the continuing influence of some European ballad traditions and the black music of the blues bars of Chicago and other American industrial cities, but in trite commercialised forms that are only a shadow of their former grandeur. A whole world of other traditions has probably been lost forever. Because we live in an isolated area, our great heritage of music and poetry has survived a little longer, but it too is dying.'

'Quite right,' said Seumas, 'art is now high art that is dead and enters the museum straight away to be revered in hushed tones, or consumer art that has to be shallow so that it will not last.'

'The eighteenth and nineteenth centuries were about increasing accessibility in the arts,' Donald argued, 'but with the arrival of the twentieth, artists and writers suddenly cried, "help! this is becoming too easy – we'll lose our pedestals", and they went in search of obscurity. Obscurity for obscurity's sake, or rather, obscurity to show how clever they were.'

'Yes and no,' said Calum. 'The twentieth century did start with the stench of intellectual snobbery, contempt for the "masses", racial superiority, eugenics, and many other things that a liberal like myself finds abhorrent. On the other hand, art and writing had come to the end of a natural cycle. They went in search of originality, not obscurity. But originality cannot be sought out, it cannot be forced, it is a by-product that is paradoxically the most important element. Often it is to be found where two cultures meet, and exists as much because of the misunderstandings between the two cultures as because of the understandings. Originality is the unconscious product of an artist's inability to understand – the sublime union of his craft and his stupidity, if his inability to live and find a settled place can be called stupidity. An artist shouldn't want to be different, he should find his difference an uncomfortable fact that he wants to overcome. Too many twentieth-century artists have gone in search of their difference, and only discovered the banality of their own meagre skills – meagre because they wanted to reject all that went before them. This trend goes back in history, and is in part due to the ever-increasing status of the artist. That status is the artist's greatest enemy.'

'Not all twentieth-century art was obsessed with originality,' said Seumas. 'A lot of art was concerned with the mass political movements of the time. Take Socialist Realism ....'

'Call that art?' scoffed Donald.

'Socialist Realism is much ridiculed for its stylistic naivety and intellectual dishonesty. This completely misses the point. The obscene thing about Socialist Realism is the uniformity of the human figure. This is shown by the paintings of Diego Rivera, whose naive style and intellectual content is not so different from Socialist Realism, and yet the individuality and humour of each of his figures make his paintings splendid monuments to a great ideal.'

' "Splendid monuments to a great ideal"! Just listen to yourself.'

'Seumas is talking sense,' Calum intervened. 'The lack of individuality and the failure to recognise the importance of individualism is at the root of much that went wrong in the politics and art of the twentieth century. We finished that century thinking there had been a victory of individualism. It is too early to say that. I think we are faced with another form of regimentation – consumerised regimentation.'

'Intellectuals saw the workers leaving the factories similarly dressed and returning to their near identical homes, and took that to mean that not only are workers identical in appearance and lifestyle, but they want to be identical,' Seumas continued the point. 'They failed to see that beneath every cloth cap there was an entirely different personality – different tastes, loves, passions, sexualities, fears and ambitions. Of course, every human being shares certain features of being a human being – that is what we have been talking about – but within those finite boundaries, those wide but finite boundaries, there is infinite variety.'

'You have mentioned your own area,' I joined the conversation after a long silence. 'Is there something particular about it?'

'Well, it has it own distinctive language and culture,' Seumas replied, 'but I don't like passing judgement on any people, least of all my own. When a people start to think themselves as hospitable, talented or simply rather nice, their collective smugness becomes unbearable.'

'That is when they cease to be hospitable, talented or simply rather nice,' said Calum.

'No people is ever more hospitable, more talented or simply rather nicer than any other people,' said Donald.

'To say that all peoples are the same is ludicrous,' observed Calum, 'because cultures have effects and a power of their own. It isn't genetic but cultural DNA that counts.'

'Right enough,' rejoined Seumas, 'all the gamut of human traits are equally distributed amongst all the peoples with the exception of the one important trait that affects all others – self-confidence. In its early stages self-confidence is a positive and liberating force. In Scotland, a country lacking in self-confidence, though perhaps it is gaining it, much of the dislike of England is based on its apparent self-confidence, though perhaps it is losing it. It is one of the greatest historical paradoxes that the only really successful revolution in the long term, that is the English one, is also the only one that is totally ignored. Following it, England became the most dynamic country in Europe. In the late-sixteenth and seventeenth centuries, its self-confidence was still tempered by a genuine sense of cultural inferiority. A very productive mix. The arrogance of empire flowered in the nineteenth century and in the century that has just ended, a pathetic lack of self-awareness appeared. This pattern is by no means confined to the English.'

'So what stage are the Americans at?' I asked.

'Arrogance of empire, I would say. And their power is much greater than any previous great power. Absolute power, they say, corrupts absolutely. It is not that the Americans are a bad people, quite the opposite: it is only in their collectivity or lack of collectivity that they have become harsh and ultimately dangerous. Americans abroad are an asset – in America as a political whole, they are a threat. If I were to be flippant, I would say give America back to its native people and send the Americans out into the world where easy smiles and New World naivety and freshness are much needed. Europe has too much history, America too little – that is their mutual attraction.'

The drunk who had been sleeping for some time sat up and tried to focus. 'Where am I?' he said. 'Edinburgh or Stornoway?'

'Stornoway', someone replied.

'Edinburgh', he insisted emphatically and syllabically.

'No, Stornoway.'

'Perhaps I should be in Edinburgh,' he muttered as a cloud of uncertainty and even a little anxiety passed over him.

'This is our Member of the Scottish Parliament,' said Calum by way of an explanation directed towards me.

This drew the drunk's attention to me and he looked at me hard, trying to concentrate on who I was. 'Do I know you?' he asked eventually.

'No, I'm just off the ferry', I replied.

'Just off the ferry', said the drunk trying to grapple with the concept.

'He's a tourist who's just arrived', explained Calum again, 'or perhaps he wouldn't thank me for the term tourist: wanderer perhaps, tramp, itinerant, drop-out or hippy. Take your pick, Angus.'

Angus the drunk looked at me hard and then swelled out his chest as though he was going to say something very important, while fully aware of the enormous effort it was going to take: 'The Catholics are just trying to be different, that's all. They used to used to be Sabbatar... they used to keep the Sabbath day too. All they want is to be different.'

'So?'

'Well, that's it, isn't it? They just want to be different. That's my point,' he repeated.

'Some of these islands are Presbyterian and some Catholic,' said Calum still providing the explanations. 'The Presbyterian islands are very strict about Sundays and the Catholic ones aren't. That's all.'

'And this is what your new parliament has got you?' I asked provocatively nodding towards the drunk.

'I would always defend our right to be ruled by our own idiots rather than anybody else's. At Westminster the English idiots always outnumber the Scottish and Welsh ones, so it is only proper that we have our own set to rule us from up here.' Calum grinned clearly offloading one of his favourite opinions.

'But not all MPs and MSPs are idiots, surely?' I said rather pedantically.

'Of course not, who do you take us for?' said Donald. 'Many are idiots, most are chancers, and some are even decent men and women. But are you always this serious? Have another dram, or is seriousness part of your nature, so with every dram you're going to get even more serious until you drive us sober with your righteousness.'

'You'll never find profundity,' Seumas advised me, 'until you've had more to drink. Profundity, as the word implies, is to be found at the bottom of the bottle and not at the top.'

I apologised with a grimace, aware of a heavy feeling of not being able to express myself. I liked my company except for Angus, the bigoted *ball parlamaid* who continued to mutter 'Just trying to be different' and 'Fuck the Pope' like a kind of rosary.

Seumas' face expressed impatience and some embarrassment. 'Strange', he said, 'how bigotry can make you defensive about the indefensible. I have little time for this Pope. The powerful are generally fairly nauseating, and this pope is no exception. But faced with this, I would defend him like a Swiss guard ... You'll have another dram?'

'Boccaccio, a Catholic priest, made this point much more cleverly,' interrupted Calum. 'He tells the story of two Florentine merchants, one Jewish and the other Christian. As they are very good friends, each wants to convert the other and save his soul. In the end the Christian starts to win the argument and the Jew prepares to convert. However, he says that before doing so, he must first visit Rome and discover how Christianity is led. Of course, his Christian friend is devastated because he knows that when the Jew sees that the seat of St Peter is infested by greed, simony, lust and every other vice, he will never consider conversion again. Yet when he returns from Rome the Jewish merchant goes straight to the cathedral and converts. His happy but confused Christian friend demands an explanation for such eccentric behaviour and the former Jew replies that when he saw the greed, the simony and the lust, he knew that only the religion chosen by God could be led so badly and still continue to prosper.'

'But all religions are like that,' said Seumas firmly. 'Like human individuals, all contain both good and bad. The good is represented by significant truths that lift humans up towards their humanity, and the bad by dishonest mystifications founded on structures of power. Religion requires organisation to survive, but organisation requires structures of power that drag religion back down.'

'Be careful of this relativism,' said Calum. 'Let me give you a political example. Movements such as socialism, whose aims I believe to be noble are similarly dragged down by the logic of human organisation, but the underlying principles still continue to have some effect. Both Hitler's Germany and Stalin's Russia were oppressively authoritarian regimes, but the victims of the former were the intended victims of a clearly racist set of beliefs, and the victims of the latter the random victims of a more complex mix of fanaticism, paranoia, intellectual intolerance, bureaucratic logic and mass hysteria. Paradoxically the irrational ideology of the former was extremely rational in the implementation of oppression, whereas the rational ideology of the latter was highly irrational in its cruelty. Little difference this made to victims of one or the other, but in the long run, communism did provide some social goods. Fascism was always going to destroy itself through its internal logic of hate. Religions like communism tend to be dragged down into the abyss of brutality by the logic of power, only to be drawn back up again by the finer aspects of their underlying beliefs.'

'Only a secularist like you,' cried Seumas, who expressed his irritation by waving Calum away with his hand while turning towards me as though in search of a more worthy interlocutor, 'could confuse religion and politics in this crass manner. Politics concerns the finite, and the merits of its various manifestations can be discussed, but their relevance barely survives a few decades. Religion on the other hand concerns the infinite, the fundamental unchanging truths of our human nature. That is why they are all without exception equally deserving of respect, and that is why they are all equally incapable of living up to their ideals. And indeed if they follow their ideals too closely they will disappear like the German Anabaptists whose pacifism allowed them to be cut down by Protestants and Catholics alike.'

Although Calum clearly enjoyed being disagreed with and liked nothing better than a good argument, he seemed a little hurt by the personal nature of Seumas' rebuttal. Seeking for once to find the compromise rather than division, he answered Seumas, 'I am unconvinced, but then as you say, a secularist like me is almost obliged to. However, I agree with the practical substance of what you say: namely that we must treat all religions with equal respect. I do so, because our little planet can no longer afford the destruction of a religious war.'

Seumas too felt more conciliatory: 'Although I firmly believe in the difference between religions and political movements, communism and Christianity shared a common source of generosity and moral outrage that only makes their crimes more tragic. The major critics, the best critics of both, were communists and Christians respectively. You would be hard pushed to find fascists who criticised their own fascist regimes on moral grounds and before those regimes started to fall apart.'

'Yes indeed,' agreed Calum, 'and the ephemeral nature of communist regimes is perhaps due to the fact that lacking a heaven in which to place their gods, they insisted on creating gods on earth. No bureaucracy can ever be so thorough and so pervasive that it can entirely protect leaders from the relentless demystification of that great and wonderful iconoclast, the historian. As it happened, Stalin, the most terrible of them all, was brought crashing down by his own party machine only a few years after his death.'

'Of course,' said Seumas gravely, 'it is not so easy at an individual level to divide the fanatic who loves all humanity from the fanatic who hates all humanity that does not belong to his or her little group, as personal motivations are always so complex. But in their extreme types, the former has a tragic quality and the latter is little more than beast.'

Angus just smiled the satisfied smile of inebriation and said: 'Fuck the Pope!'

The stubborn bigotry expressed by Angus' considered opinion brought the religious part of our discussion to an abrupt halt. Seumas turned to me with a smile and said, 'Join us in finding that brief glimpse of truth that comes from scattered thoughts gently polished up with a little drink.'

I hesitated at the idea of more strong liquor. It had cost me so many moments of embarrassment, so much loss of self-esteem, and so little real fun, or at least fun that could be remembered. Drink had landed me up against the murderous vet, in the hands of thugs, and fogged the erudition of my sojourn in academic circles. The nightmare of hallucination and depression in my early life had been marked out by the sound of empty bottles thudding stupidly on the carpet – the dark dreams of desire and guilt used to swell like a black cloud foaming in a Hebridean sky. 'I don't think I'll drink any more. I am apt to do stupid things and believe them even more stupid the next day.'

'You feel guilty the day after a night on the batter?'

'Yes'

'A definite case of an over-inflated super-ego, I would say', said Donald and he went off to the bar.

'What's a super-ego?' said the drunk.

'It could be a name for you, Angus,' said Seumas, 'given the size of your ego'.

'There never was any sense to hanging on,' said Calum, 'to all that self-control. Guilt has a place, but don't turn it into a way of life, don't torture yourself for little things. We've all made fools of ourselves. Some people have even built careers out of making fools of themselves, isn't that right Angus.'

'Fools?' said the drunk looking around carefully, as though trying to pick one out. 'Fools? Who's acting the fool?'

As laughter spread, Donald reappeared, handed me a whisky and said, '*Sin agad e, a bhalaich*, relax and just join in the crack. Don't put too much store by either mirth or sobriety – both are affectations. Sit back and enjoy the moment of it. The past and the future are merely perceptions, chemically controlled perceptions, and that stuff helps. I know, I've done all the clinical tests.'

His words reminded me of the mirth-worshippers, the fanatical followers of Bacchus, who made such a fool of me, who turned my mind with their hellish prank. Perhaps he was right; perhaps by reacting against the craving for shallow laughter and consumable pleasure, I had turned myself into a dull, overly thoughtful and anally retentive moralist incapable of doing anything when anything I could do would only be insignificant and lost in the sea of human actions, the multitude of useful and useless acts that drop into the abyss of forgetfulness.

'Thanks,' I said, 'I probably could do with one.'

At that moment, the two drunks, the pleasant and the unpleasant, stood up to leave. When they reached the door, as though by sudden inspiration, he started to grope her greedily. She simply elbowed him in the stomach and disappeared into the night. He then pulled his middle-aged face into a childish expression, and slowly turned back towards us, as though he had something to say. But he appeared to think the better of it, or perhaps he simply forgot his words – his mouth shut, he turned again and he too disappeared into the night. That was his goodbye. To me they seemed an inebriated version of the vulture chasing the dove, death chasing life and love, and Bacchus chasing the young woman. The one destined to shabby success and the other to heroic failure.

We spoke long into the night. I asked them what could be the role of the periphery in the coming century. Seumas confidently replied that, while the cities, the large cosmopolitan cities, had been the engines of change in the nineteenth and twentieth centuries, now the periphery was about to take over. Only the periphery retains the proper measure of man, he claimed. Donald, on the other hand, was very pessimistic. The centre would continue to destroy the periphery – that was an economic fact. For him, the periphery is only a place to escape to, precisely because it has no relevance. Calum was less categorical in his opinion, and suggested that only fools engage in prophesy, but anyway the centre and the periphery would probably continue to influence each other, though the balance of power might shift slightly.

We went our separate ways, and I to the shore, the periphery of the periphery. The waves slapped at the rounded stones rhythmically and endlessly. They seemed to pulse with the pace of my own drink-laden head. I was alone at the edge of a vast sea that hung like death beyond those insignificant stones, each an individual in shape, colour and texture, but nevertheless very similar. While the sea ebbed and eddied eternity, the beach collected the detritus of the modern world. Of the plastic containers, some were relatively new and still proclaimed what their shortlived use had been, others were bleached by the joint efforts of sun and sea. Eternity was still eternity, but from now on it would be a polluted one.

The expectant and yet unhurried sea that slowly erodes the shore resembles death that erodes the living and sucks them into a grey and formless sleep. As it rushed in and then pulled back gurgling incessantly, the sea seemed to draw me in. I stared at it for a long time and wondered if there would be any pleasure in its cold grasp.

* * * * *

I realise that I may have stretched the reader's credulity to its limits. I will not say where I have plundered the plots of others. Those who carry the burden of their hard-won erudition, will recognise them easily enough. Those who carry the equally heavy burden of their instinctive common-sense will be freer to form their own opinions. They may say, and their common sense will indeed tell them so, that it is absurd that men should turn into animals and that animals that speak are strictly for fairy tales, but they cannot deny that every day men and women turn into animals in a truer and more dramatic manner than in any metamorphosis I have described. Now the distance that divides us from the animals does not seem so dramatic. The distance is now between the individual and the 'mass'. Don't get me wrong, I'm as slobbish as the next man and happy to be so, but like all filthy egalitarians, I can't help feeling we lost something significant when we lost our sense of superiority as a species. That held us together, and one humanism led to the other.

Forgive me if I have not been precise, if I have not ended with a clear 'What Is' and 'What Should Be'. I can only speak in the language of our age and we are all word-weary and idea-idle; we have eaten rich food and lack the clarity that comes with want.

We are often incapable of saying what is really important and what we can say changes in the saying. We throw it out, a fragment of our limited experience and it is caught by others whose limited experiences are unlikely to be the same as ours, although possibly very similar. They can catch it on the wing as a child catches a butterfly in the cup of his hands and immediately lets it go, holding it just time enough to feel the superficial but energetic flap-flap of fragile wings, or they can net it, study it, inspect its colours, categorise its species and pierce its living body with a pin. To weigh words up is to change their meanings. We are forced to give importance to what we can express, hoping there aren't too many word-weighing pedants, who will interpret them in the dusty laboratory of their reason and not in the summer light of what we could not really know but only feel.

Some other books published by **LUATH** PRESS

FICTION

Six Black Candles
Des Dillon
ISBN 1 84282 053 2 PB £6.99

Me and Ma Gal
Des Dillon
ISBN 1 84282 054 0 PB £5.99

Driftnet
Lin Anderson
ISBN 1 84282 034 6 PB £9.99

The Fundamentals of New Caledonia
David Nicol
ISBN 1 84282 93 6 HB £16.99

Milk Treading
Nick Smith
ISBN 1 84282 037 0 PB £6.99

The Road Dance
John MacKay
ISBN 1 84282 040 0 PB £6.99

The Strange Case of RL Stevenson
Richard Woodhead
ISBN 0 946487 86 3 HB £16.99

But n Ben A-Go-Go
Matthew Fitt
ISBN 0 946487 82 0 HB £10.99
ISBN 1 84282 014 1 PB £6.99

The Bannockburn Years
William Scott
ISBN 0 946487 34 0 PB £7.95

Outlandish Affairs: An Anthology of Amorous Encounters
Edited and introduced by Evan Rosenthal and Amanda Robinson
ISBN 1 84282 055 9 PB £9.99

The Tar Factory
Alan Kelly
ISBN 1 84282 050 8 PB £9.99

Grave Robbers
Robin Mitchell
ISBN 0 946487 72 3 PB £7.99

The Great Melnikov
Hugh MacLachlan
ISBN 0 946487 42 1 PB £7.95

POETRY

Tartan & Turban
Bashabi Fraser
ISBN 1 84282 044 3 PB £8.99

Drink the Green Fairy
Brian Whittingham
ISBN 1 84282 045 1 PB £8.99

Talking with Tongues
Brian D. Finch
ISBN 1 84282 006 0 PB £8.99

Kate o Shanter's Tale and other poems [book]
Matthew Fitt
ISBN 1 84282 028 1 PB £6.99

Kate o Shanter's Tale and other poems [audio CD]
Matthew Fitt
ISBN 1 84282 043 5 CD £9.99

Bad Ass Raindrop
Kokumo Rocks
ISBN 1 84282 018 4 PB £6.99

Madame Fifi's Farewell and other poems
Gerry Cambridge
ISBN 1 84282 005 2 PB £8.99

Poems to be Read Aloud
introduced by Tom Atkinson
ISBN 0 946487 00 6 PB £5.00

Scots Poems to be Read Aloud
introduced by Stuart McHardy
ISBN 0 946487 81 2 PB £5.00

Picking Brambles
Des Dillon
ISBN 1 84282 021 4 PB £6.99

Sex, Death & Football
Alistair Findlay
ISBN 1 84282 022 2 PB £6.99

The Luath Burns Companion
John Cairney
ISBN 1 84282 000 1 PB £10.00

Immortal Memories: A Compilation of Toasts to the Memory of Burns as delivered at Burns Suppers, 1801-2001
John Cairney
ISBN 1 84282 009 5 HB £20.00

The Whisky Muse: Scotch whisky in poem & song
Robin Laing
ISBN 1 84282 041 9 PB £7.99

The Ruba'iyat of Omar Khayyam, in Scots
Rab Wilson
ISBN 1 84282 046 X PB £8.99

Men and Beasts: Wild Men and Tame Animals
Valerie Gillies and Rebecca Marr
ISBN 0 946487 928 PB £15.00

FOLKLORE

Scotland: Myth, Legend & Folklore
Stuart McHardy
ISBN 0 946487 69 3 PB £7.99

Luath Storyteller: Highland Myths & Legends
George W Macpherson
ISBN 1 84282 003 6 PB £5.00

Tales of the North Coast
Alan Temperley
ISBN 0 946487 18 9 PB £8.99

Tall Tales from an Island
Peter Macnab
ISBN 0 946487 07 3 PB £8.99

The Supernatural Highlands
Francis Thompson
ISBN 0 946487 31 6 PB £8.99

THE QUEST FOR

The Quest for Robert Louis Stevenson
John Cairney
ISBN 0 946487 87 1 HB £16.99

The Quest for the Nine Maidens
Stuart McHardy
ISBN 0 946487 66 9 HB £16.99

The Quest for the Original Horse Whisperers
Russell Lyon
ISBN 1 842820 020 6 HB £16.99

The Quest for the Celtic Key
Karen Ralls-MacLeod and
Ian Robertson
ISBN 1 842820 031 1 PB £8.99

The Quest for Arthur
Stuart McHardy
ISBN 1 842820 12 5 HB £16.99

ON THE TRAIL OF

On the Trail of William Wallace
David R Ross
ISBN 0 946487 47 2 PB £7.99

On the Trail of Robert the Bruce
David R Ross
ISBN 0 946487 52 9 PB £7.99

On the Trail of Mary Queen of Scots
J Keith Cheetham
ISBN 0 946487 50 2 PB £7.99

On the Trail of Bonnie Prince Charlie
David R Ross
ISBN 0 946487 68 5 PB £7.99

On the Trail of Robert Burns
John Cairney
ISBN 0 946487 51 0 PB £7.99

On the Trail of John Muir
Cherry Good
ISBN 0 946487 62 6 PB £7.99

On the Trail of Queen Victoria in the Highlands
Ian R Mitchell
ISBN 0 946487 79 0 PB £7.99

On the Trail of Robert Service
G Wallace Lockhart
ISBN 0 946487 24 3 PB £7.99

On the Trail of the Pilgrim Fathers
J Keith Cheetham
ISBN 0 946487 83 9 PB £7.99

LUATH GUIDES TO SCOTLAND

The North West Highlands: Roads to the Isles
Tom Atkinson
ISBN 0 946487 54 5 PB £4.95

Mull and Iona: Highways and Byways
Peter Macnab
ISBN 0 946487 58 8 PB £4.95

The Northern Highlands: The Empty Lands
Tom Atkinson
ISBN 0 946487 55 3 PB £4.95

The West Highlands: The Lonely Lands
Tom Atkinson
ISBN 0 946487 56 1 PB £4.95

HISTORY

Scots in Canada
Jenni Calder
ISBN 1 84282 038 9 PB £7.99

Civil Warrior
Robin Bell
ISBN 1 84282 013 3 HB £10.99

A Passion for Scotland
David R Ross
ISBN 1 84282 019 2 PB £5.99

Reportage Scotland
Louise Yeoman
ISBN 0 946487 61 8 PB £9.99

Plaids & Bandanas: Highland Drover to Wild West Cowboy
Rob Gibson
ISBN 0 946487 88 X PB £7.99

POLITICS & CURRENT ISSUES

Scotlands of the Mind
Angus Calder
ISBN 1 84282 008 7 PB £9.99

Trident on Trial: the case for people's disarmament
Angie Zelter
ISBN 1 84282 004 4 PB £9.99

Uncomfortably Numb: A Prison Requiem
Maureen Maguire
ISBN 1 84282 001 X PB £8.99

Scotland: Land & Power – Agenda for Land Reform
Andy Wightman
ISBN 0 946487 70 7 PB £5.00

Old Scotland New Scotland
Jeff Fallow
ISBN 0 946487 40 5 PB £6.99

Some Assembly Required: behind the scenes at the rebirth of the Scottish Parliament
David Shepherd
ISBN 0 946487 84 7 PB £7.99

Notes from the North
Emma Wood
ISBN 0 946487 46 4 PB £8.99

NATURAL WORLD

The Hydro Boys: pioneers of renewable energy
Emma Wood
ISBN 1 84282 016 8 HB £16.99

Wild Scotland
James McCarthy
ISBN 0 946487 37 5 PB £8.99

Wild Lives: Otters – On the Swirl of the Tide
Bridget MacCaskill
ISBN 0 946487 67 7 PB £9.99

Wild Lives: Foxes – The Blood is Wild
Bridget MacCaskill
ISBN 0 946487 71 5 PB £9.99

Scotland – Land & People: An Inhabited Solitude
James McCarthy
ISBN 0 946487 57 X PB £7.99

The Highland Geology Trail
John L Roberts
ISBN 0 946487 36 7 PB £4.99

Red Sky at Night
John Barrington
ISBN 0 946487 60 X PB £8.99

Listen to the Trees
Don MacCaskill
ISBN 0 946487 65 0 PB £9.99

SOCIAL HISTORY

Pumpherston: the story of a shale oil village
Sybil Cavanagh
ISBN 1 84282 011 7 HB £17.99
ISBN 1 84282 015 X PB £10.99

Shale Voices
Alistair Findlay
ISBN 0 946487 78 2 HB £17.99
ISBN 0 946487 48 0 PB £10.99

A Word for Scotland
Jack Campbell
ISBN 0 946487 48 0 PB £12.99

BIOGRAPHY

The Last Lighthouse
Sharma Krauskopf
ISBN 0 946487 96 0 PB £7.99

Tobermory Teuchter
Peter Macnab
ISBN 0 946487 41 3 PB £7.99

Bare Feet and Tackety Boots
Archie Cameron
ISBN 0 946487 17 0 PB £7.95

Come Dungeons Dark
John Taylor Caldwell
ISBN 0 946487 19 7 PB £6.95